"Don't . . . Don't You Dare Touch Me!"

Ann cried.

"You can't handle it, can you?" Drew taunted.

"No, I guess I can't," she answered dully.

"Can't or don't want to?" His penetrating blue eyes seemed to read her soul.

"Maybe a little of both."

"I see."

"No, I don't think you do."

A muscle in his cheek throbbed. "If I'd thought something like this would happen, I never would have had you come. But the way I see it, life's one big gamble, anyway."

"Not to me it isn't."

He smiled coldly. "You're right about that. If it's not a sure thing, you aren't interested. You're a coward, Ann Sinclair."

"That's not true!" she countered.

"Yes, it is. The thought of taking a chance absolutely blows your mind. The bottom line is, you're afraid."

Dear Reader,

Joan Hohl is back! And I know you're all cheering at her return. Her *Man of the Month* book, *Convenient Husband,* is Joan at her steamiest, and her hero, Jasper (also known as "Main") Chance, is a man to remember. That's *all* I'm going to tell you about this sexy, sensuous story.... You'll just have to read it for yourself.

A book by Lass Small is always a treat, and you'll all be thrilled to know that *A Restless Man* is the first in her three-book series about those Fabulous Brown Brothers. (Yes, you first met Bob Brown in her 1991 *Man of the Month* book, *'Twas the Night.*) Look for more of the Brown men in October and December.

August is completed with a terrific story from Mary Lynn Baxter, *And Baby Makes Perfect* (another hero to remember!); *Just Like Old Times* by Jennifer Greene (watch out for the matchmaking teenagers!); *Midsummer Madness* by Christine Rimmer (with Cody McIntyre, town hunk); and *Sarah and the Stranger* by Shawna Delacorte, a new author you'll hear more of.

Next month, look for Silhouette Desire books by some of your favorite authors, including Annette Broadrick, Diana Palmer and Helen R. Myers.

All the best,

Lucia Macro
Senior Editor

MARY LYNN BAXTER

AND BABY MAKES PERFECT

SILHOUETTE *Desire*®

Published by Silhouette Books New York

America's Publisher of Contemporary Romance

SILHOUETTE BOOKS
300 East 42nd St., New York, N.Y. 10017

AND BABY MAKES PERFECT

ISBN: 0-373-05727-X

First Silhouette Books printing August 1992

Printed in the U.S.A.

MARY LYNN BAXTER

sold hundreds of romances before she ever wrote one. The D & B Bookstore, right on the main drag in Lufkin, Texas, is the store she owns and manages. She and her husband, Leonard, garden in their spare time. Around five o'clock every evening they can be found picking butter beans on their small farm just outside of town.

Prologue

———

Sweat trickled down his face, but Drew MacMillan failed to notice or to care until the liquid dripped into his mouth. He grimaced; the sour taste forced him to lift the tail of his T-shirt and swipe at his lips. Still, his concentration held as he stared at the newspaper article.

> Houston's most eligible bachelor, Drew MacMillan, strikes out again. Engagement #2 has apparently been called off by his fiancée. Could the automobile magnate and racer be less than perfect, after all? Mmm, stay tuned....

"Damn," Drew muttered, his features twisted into a scowl. Gossip columns. They ought to be outlawed, he thought. Furthermore, someone ought to shoot the people who wrote them, this one in particular.

Yet he, like scores of others on Sunday morning, found himself reading the fat, juicy column.

Drew had awakened around seven and decided it would be blasphemy to pass up the opportunity to jog on this spring morning. April rarely saw a cool morning, and even though he normally didn't exercise on Sunday, he'd made the exception today.

He'd enjoyed the three-mile run, especially since the dogwood trees and purple wisteria were in full bloom. He appreciated the finer things in life only when he ran; most of the time he was so busy that nature's beauty passed him by.

Though dripping wet, he'd walked through the side door of his southwest Houston condo completely relaxed, his thoughts on a meeting he would have later that day with his assistant to discuss an important business deal. He'd taken a quick shower, slipped into a T-shirt and pair of athletic shorts, then grabbed a cup of coffee.

He'd sat down at the kitchen table and spread the paper. He hadn't been in the mood to read the society page, but something had drawn his gaze, a premonition maybe. When his name had leapt out at him, he'd frozen inside, as if he'd been zapped with an electrical shock.

Now, as he reread the insulting words, Drew pushed back from the table, snatched the sheet containing the article, wadded the page into a tiny ball and tossed it into the nearest trash can. Garbage, pure and simple.

For starters, his fiancée hadn't broken the engagement, *he* had.

Drew reached for his cup and took a sip of the now tepid coffee. He muttered another expletive, only to then hear a tap on the back door.

Before he could say anything, the door opened and his assistant, Skip Howard, sauntered over the threshold.

Skip took one look at Drew's face and grinned. "What's got you so riled? You look like you just bit into an apple and found a worm."

Drew's brows furrowed into a deeper frown. "Funny."

"Wasn't meant to be."

Drew felt the tight coil around his belly loosen. "You're right. I did just bite into the apple—and I found the worm."

Skip laughed. "Wanna explain?"

Skip, a crackerjack second-in-command, was also a good friend. Drew respected and admired him because of his integrity and his loyalty.

To look at Skip, though, the word ordinary or nondescript jumped to mind. Everything about the man was average. Average height, average weight and average features. His deep chestnut-colored hair and heavy-lidded eyes even looked average on him. But you had to be around him only a short time before you realized there was nothing average about his mind or his sharp and sometimes caustic wit. When Skip spoke, Drew paid attention.

"You still haven't answered my question."

Drew pointed toward the trash.

Skip moved to the brass container and peered inside. "I don't see anything except maybe a spit wad."

Drew laughed a humorless laugh.

Skip shrugged, then leaned down and retrieved the paper. While he read it, Drew poured Skip a cup of coffee and set it on the table. But Drew was too restless to sit down. He propped himself against the cabinet and watched from under hooded eyes for his friend's reaction.

Finally Skip looked up, a wide grin once again fixed on his face.

"What the hell's so funny?"

Skip's grin fled. "Nothing really. It's just that you're so uptight."

"Wouldn't you be?"

"Yeah, guess so. The lady doesn't pull any punches, does she?"

"Think I've got grounds for a suit?"

Skip reached for his coffee without taking his eyes off Drew. "Why don't you lighten up, take it in stride? The publicity's good for your image."

"That's bull and you know it. That broad has attacked me personally, and I sure as hell don't want her to get away with it."

Skip lifted his shoulders in another shrug. "When you're in the limelight you should expect this kind of stuff."

Drew couldn't argue. Thanks to hard work, his two Jaguar dealerships in Texas and one in Louisiana were booming. His success had enabled him to do what he really wanted and that was race cars. His racetrack skills, combined with his reputation as a ladies' man, made him fair game for the press.

"So you think I ought to leave well enough alone, huh?"

Skip stretched his legs out in front of him and crossed his arms over his chest. "Sure do."

Drew thrust a hand through his sandy-colored hair. "What if it doesn't blow over? What if she thinks she can take potshots at me anytime she wants to and get away with it?"

"If she does, then you just might have to do something about it. Until then, my advice is just to ignore it and see if interest in you dies a natural death."

Drew knew Skip was right. Nevertheless, it galled him to sit by and let the columnist get away with what amounted to slander. Maybe Skip was right, though, and he was making a mountain out of a molehill. He'd be the first to admit that he had a low boiling point, that things got to him in the worst sort of way. But incompetence made him see red. And that lady gossip columnist was as incompetent as hell for not getting her facts straight before she printed them.

"I guess it's safe to say, you're not in the mood to discuss business?"

Skip's brisk voice snapped Drew back to the moment at hand. "No, but I don't have much choice. We can't keep Blackwell Realty waiting much longer. If we don't give them an answer soon, we'll lose the property."

Skip leaned down and reached for his briefcase. "It's a good deal, Drew, in spite of the price."

"I don't know." Drew bent over the papers that Skip spread across the table. "What if we decide not to put another dealership in Texas? I sure don't want to be stuck with the property."

"But—"

The phone rang. Drew got up and crossed the room to the buffet where it sat and lifted the receiver.

As he listened, his face turned a pasty white.

"What's wrong?" Skip demanded.

"It's John, my daddy."

"On the phone?"

Drew grimaced as he hung up. "No. That was the family doctor."

"Uh-oh, bad news."

"John's had a stroke."

"Hey, man, I'm sorry."

"Yeah, me too," Drew said, his voice lifeless.

Skip stood and gathered his papers. "Well, don't worry about things here. If the Blackwells don't want to wait for an answer, then to hell with them. You go ahead and do what you have to do." Skip paused. "Is there anything I can do?"

"No," Drew said. "Thanks."

Skip walked to the door. "Let me hear."

"Yeah."

"You sure you're all right?"

Drew nodded. "I'm fine."

Skip looked as if he wanted to argue, but he didn't. Instead, he opened the door and walked out.

Drew stood rigid, his hands balled into fists. He didn't want to go home. He was concerned about his daddy, but there was no love lost between them. He'd be the first to admit that and his daddy second. Still, that didn't alter the fact that he had to return home to MacMillan, Texas. He had his mother to think about. And he loved her very much.

He turned and headed for his bedroom to pack his bags. Dread weighted his footsteps.

One

"**I**f you want *my* opinion, I think he can't get it up."
Ignoring the startling silence in the nail shop, and the
uncertain giggles, Hazel Minshew went on, "Oh,
what's that word?" She pursed her lips and she
flapped her hand, well aware that she was center stage,
and loving it. "*Impotent*—that's it."

Ann Sinclair tried to control the shock waves that
coursed through her, but she couldn't. Her hand
shook to such an extent that the polish applicator in
her hand slid up Jewell Thornton's fat finger.

"Oh!" Jewell cried, horrified.

Color flooded Ann's face as her eyes locked on the
splash of Positively Red nail polish that covered all of
Jewell's finger. For a moment Ann couldn't seem to
move, appalled at her lack of control.

Pauline Sims, also waiting her turn for a manicure, laughed out loud. "Goodness, Ann, I don't think I've ever seen you so flustered." She lowered her voice conspiratorially. "Us talking about Drew MacMillan wouldn't have anything to do with it, now would it?"

Before Ann could reply, Sophie Renfro, her employee and friend said, "Hey, Pauline, cut it out. You know how Ann feels about gossip, especially the garbage-can variety."

Ann cast Sophie a grateful glance while she doused two cotton balls with remover and vigorously rubbed Jewell's hand.

When Drew MacMillan's name had been brought up initially, Ann had made it a point to distance herself from the conversation. She did in fact abhor gossip and always tried her best to control it in its earliest stages. But she wasn't successful all the time; today proved that.

"Why, that's the silliest thing I've ever heard," Pauline added, batting her black false eyelashes. "I can't imagine Drew MacMillan not being able to get a hard-on."

Ann knew beauty parlors and nail shops were hotbeds for idle gossip. When she'd opened Polished Choice several years ago, she'd been determined her shop was going to be different. For the most part, it had been.

Maybe if she pointedly continued to ignore the women, they would cease discussing Drew's sex life, of all things.

"Makes sense to me," Hazel said, waving the society-page article through the air. "Why else can't he keep a woman?"

"Oh, for heaven's sake, Hazel. Get real." Both of Pauline's eyelashes were slapping her upper cheeks. "I imagine Drew's just the opposite. Why I bet he's randy as hell."

If the situation hadn't been so serious, Ann would have laughed, fully expecting at least one set of Pauline's eyelashes to pop off from sheer overexertion. But the situation was serious. Enough was enough.

"Okay, ladies," Ann said. "You've had your say and your fun. If you don't mind, I think you've raked Drew MacMillan over the coals enough. Anyway, you all know the stuff that's in the news is not worth the paper it's printed on. It's gossip and that's all. Besides, Drew MacMillan is not a topic I want discussed in my shop."

Though she spoke in her usual soft, modulated voice, there was a hint of steel behind it. Everyone heard it and wasn't about to ignore her. When Ann's violet-colored eyes darkened and her jaw clenched, she meant business.

She'd much rather concentrate on her good fortunes than the MacMillan family. She gazed around the shop and smiled to herself.

She had worked hard to obtain the success she now enjoyed as the only licensed manicurist in a town the size of MacMillan. In fact it was almost unheard of. When she'd conceived the idea, naysayers had voiced their opinions loud and clear.

"You're crazy. MacMillan's not large enough to support such a venture."

"You'll lose your shirt, young lady, just as sure as it rains buckets in East Texas."

Ann had ignored those comments and a dozen others like them, determined that MacMillan, along with the neighboring counties, could support her shop.

Thanks to the MacMillans, MacMillan, Texas, was a well-heeled town of approximately five thousand. The town bore the MacMillan name because the family owned the majority of the land that comprised it. Along with the newspaper and the grocery/hardware store, a large lumber company provided the community's lifeblood. Combined, those businesses made MacMillan prosperous.

Ann's success, however, hadn't come easily. She had overcome great odds, the main one being her poor background. She had been reared in a home where money was short but love was abundant.

The latter hadn't been enough for her brother, Peter, who was ashamed that his parents were employed by the MacMillans. Alice Sinclair had labored as a maid, while Burton had worked as a gardener and general handyman.

Even so, Peter and Drew had been best friends. Ann, two years older, used to envy her brother. She'd had a secret crush on Drew—thought he was the handsomest boy she had ever seen. But he'd never known she was alive except as Peter's older sister.

Despite the pain and heartache the MacMillans later brought to bear on her family, Ann didn't hold grudges. Well...maybe a slight grudge against John

MacMillan. In fact, she wasn't sure she could ever forgive him. But Drew was a different matter altogether.

Ann sometimes wondered if she hadn't carried that schoolgirl crush into womanhood, only to dismiss the thought as both ridiculous and ludicrous.

"You're right, of course, Ann," Pauline said, bridging the long silence and breaking into Ann's thoughts, the lines around her eyes easing somewhat under her smile. "We ought to be ashamed, especially with John lying ill in the hospital."

Another moment of silence followed, as the ladies weighed the changes that would affect the town, and their livelihoods, should something happen to John MacMillan.

"I would've never thought it, but my nails look great," Jewell said, eyeing Ann carefully, as if trying to read what went on behind that reserved but warm facade.

The entire time Ann had been woolgathering, she had automatically put a second coat of polish on Jewell's nails, followed by the top coat. Now she was about to put solar oil on them to seal the polish and moisten the cuticles.

Ann smiled. "I'm glad you're pleased. I know you don't want to hear this, but next week I'll probably have to cut them or you're going to lose two, that I know of, on your right hand."

Jewell's lips puckered. "If I lose even one before the country-club dance this weekend, I'll just die."

Ann knew that if she looked at Sophie, she would burst out laughing. Sophie's eyes were sure to be facing heavenward.

Keeping a straight face was hard to do, especially when Hazel put in scathingly, "Cool it. No one's going to notice whether you lose a fingernail or not."

"I don't know about y'all, but I'm tired of paying so much for groceries." Only after Sophie smoothly changed the subject did the ladies settle down.

"Whew, I don't know about you, but I'm exhausted," Sophie said an hour later. It was after five o'clock, and the shop had closed for the day. "Those three women drive me up the wall."

Ann had just cleaned her station and treated herself to a mug of coffee. She'd had two sips, but they had failed to buoy her spirits.

She focused her attention outside. She found that looking at the glories of springtime cheered her. The park across the street had more than its fair share of huge oak trees, their branches forming odd, irregular patterns. Beneath them, annuals carpeted the ground in a blaze of color.

Sophie chuckled. 'I thought I'd lose it for sure when you smeared that polish all over Jewell's fat hand.' Sophie's chuckle burgeoned into full laughter. "Tell you the truth, I loved it."

A smile toyed with Ann's lips. "You're bad, my friend."

"I know."

"Thanks for siding with me."

Always, Ann thought. She wouldn't have made it this far without Sophie's help and support. Sophie worked hard, then at the end of the day went home to her three-year-old whom she alone supported, thanks to a husband who had abandoned her when she got pregnant.

But Ann knew her friend wasn't destined to stay single much longer. With her fiery red hair, pixie features and mischievous brown eyes, she never lacked for male companionship.

"Hey, no way could I sit back and let them rip apart a hunk like Drew MacMillan. Why he's..."

Ann's smile faded.

"Sorry," Sophie said, an odd look in her eyes. After a brief pause, she went on, "Look, considering how close we've become since I've been working for you, don't you think it's time you leveled with me, told me what the deal is between you and the Mac-Millans?"

"It's not a pretty story," Ann said with a sigh.

"I'd still like to hear it."

Ann's words came slowly. "You know that both my parents worked for the MacMillans."

Sophie nodded.

"And my brother, Peter, and Drew were close. Anyway, Drew loved cars, and because he had money, he had a fast, powerful car, which he loved. The faster, the better."

Ann paused again and leaned tiredly against the window ledge. "One afternoon after football practice, Peter was in the car with Drew when a truck ran a stop sign."

Sophie sucked in her breath.

Ann continued, a faraway look in her eyes. "Drew slammed into the side of the truck, and though Drew wasn't hurt, Peter was."

"God, what a mess."

"You don't know the half. Drew was absolved of any wrongdoing, but Peter blamed him for the knee damage that ended his dream of playing pro ball."

"A crying shame."

"Peter never recovered and is still a big problem."

"And something happened to your daddy, right?" Sophie flushed and looked slightly embarrassed. "I have to admit that when I first came here, I heard some gossip—"

Ann held up her hand. "Don't apologize. For the longest time, the Sinclair scandal was the hot topic of conversation." She didn't curb the bitterness that laced her words.

"What happened?" Sophie pressed gently.

"Shortly after the accident, John accused my daddy of stealing, then fired him. Though my daddy was later found innocent, the damage had been done." Ann blinked back tears.

"Look, if this is too painful—"

"Not too long afterward, Daddy...took his own life."

The room fell ominously silent.

Sophie gnawed the inside of her lips. "Oh, Ann, honey, how horrible."

"Yeah, it was a bit much to handle," Ann said, and dabbed at the tears with her fingertips. "But it happened a long time ago, and as the old saying goes, 'time is a great healer.'"

"Look, why don't we stop by Sam's and get something to eat? Maybe it'll put a little color back in your cheeks."

Ann smiled wanly. "Thanks, but no thanks. If you don't mind, I think I'll go home, take a hot bath and go to bed."

"Well, if you're sure—"

"I'm sure. You go on. I'll talk to you later."

Fifteen minutes later, Ann locked the door behind her and headed home. *Home.* That word should have made her feel better. It didn't. Her thoughts were too chaotic. Talking about the past, about Drew, had upset her far more than she cared to admit.

Would he come home to check on his daddy? If so, would she see him?

Two

Ann opened the door to her house with her mind still churning. A much-craved sense of peace settled over her, and she smiled.

The small, but adorable, house, with its living room and attached kitchen, fireplace, two bedrooms and two baths, belonged to her. That wasn't exactly true, she corrected mentally. The mortgage company had its fair share. But she was confident that one day her home would belong to her.

The living area had high ceilings and many windows. Sunlight flooded through the glass, expanding the dimensions of the room. However, its spaciousness gave way to an ordered clutter. Live plants, shelves of books, bric-a-brac and family pictures were scattered about the room, along with framed prints on the wall, a flowered, overstuffed couch and several inviting chairs.

An air of coziness prevailed that suited Ann just fine and fitted her long-range plans. One day, the spare bedroom would belong to the baby she had hopes of adopting. Ann wrapped her arms around herself and squeezed, a feeling of excitement sweeping over her.

A baby. A real live human being. Her baby. Hugging that sweet thought, she scurried into her bedroom, dumped her purse and briefcase, then kicked off her shoes.

Her feet sank into the soft, seafoam-green carpet as she made her way to the closet. A few minutes later, she shed her skirt and blouse for a pair of walking shorts and cotton shirt.

She padded back into the kitchen and helped herself to a glass of iced tea from the fridge. A ton of paperwork awaited her, but for the moment, she aimed to sit and enjoy the peace and quiet.

She loved her job and couldn't wait to get to work, but the constant chatter often got on her nerves. She considered herself a "people person," yet a side of her coveted the time she was alone.

She walked into the living room and sat on the sofa. She curled her feet under her and was about to sip her tea when the phone rang. Her heart jumped as it always did, especially when she was at home. For days, she'd been expecting a call from the state adoption agency; she had filled out the preliminary application one month ago.

With shaking hands, she lifted the receiver. "Hello," she said.

"Ms. Sinclair?"

"Yes?"

"This is Dorothy Sable at the state agency."

"Oh."

The woman's voice held amusement as if she expected that reaction. "I'm calling to let you know that your application has been placed in the 'active file.'"

"Oh," Ann said again, then felt like an idiot for her tongue-tied behavior.

Dorothy Sable chuckled warmly.

"That means my name has been actually placed on the list?" Ann asked in a surprisingly strong voice.

"Exactly. The next step is an orientation meeting here in Austin."

"That's wonderful."

"So the next contact I have with you will be to set a date and time for that meeting."

"All . . . right."

"Any questions?" Ms. Sable asked, that warmth still present in her tone.

"Can you give me an idea how long the wait will be?" Ann asked.

"No, I'm sorry I can't."

"Thanks for calling," Ann said.

"I'll be in touch, then. Goodbye."

Ann reached for a decorator pillow and squeezed it. Her heart hammered so fast, she thought she might faint.

Reality hit. Was this something she really wanted to do? A panicked feeling upped her heart rate even higher. Did she know what she was getting into? Was she prepared for the upheaval a baby would bring?

Was she willing to make adjustments in her way of life, alter it to fit a baby's needs? Was she willing to give up her independence?

"Yes, yes, yes!" she whispered aloud, struggling to ward off the tears.

She took several deep breaths and cautioned herself against getting too excited or getting her hopes up. Not only was the waiting period interminable, but the odds of the adoption actually happening remained chancy, despite the active status of her application.

Single-parent adoptions were uphill battles, or as Sophie had put it, "They're no piece of cake." Certainly such adoptions were not looked on favorably because the demand for newborn babies far outweighed the supply. She knew that. Too, she must keep in mind the orientation and home visit. They were both crucial. She mustn't loose sight of either of those variables.

Yet she couldn't squelch the excitement that made her slightly giddy. But she was scared. Lord was she ever.

What would it be like to be a mother? Would she botch the job? Would the missing male figure cause her to rear a dysfunctional child? How would the lack be felt? The thought beat like a dull throb inside her, like a bone bruise that wouldn't heal.

Still, she knew she had to try. Why? Her life was remarkably on track, considering what she had suffered. But she wanted more. She wanted someone to love.

Following her daddy's suicide, she'd had to glue her shattered heart and soul back together piece by piece.

She'd also had the responsibility of helping her mother regroup. When it had become feasible to leave her mother, she'd gone to Tyler and enrolled in business school, only to find that she didn't like it.

One of her college friends had suggested she try beauty school—in light of the fact that she was continually cutting and fixing someone's hair. The thought had excited Ann, and after enrolling, she found she loved it. She also found she liked giving manicures even more, challenged by the opportunity of transforming ugly hands and nails into beautiful ones, like hers. She'd been blessed with slender fingers and long, strong nails, which drew envious comments.

After she'd returned to MacMillan and worked as a beautician, she longed to own her own shop. That had been neither feasible nor practical as her mother had become stricken with cancer. The responsibility to care for her had fallen on Ann's shoulders. Her brother had been no help. She had worked as well as nursed her mother until her death.

Ann had put in longer, more grueling hours at work to fill the void, and soon had managed to save enough money to rent a building and set herself up in business.

Her shop had done so well that now she was in the process of expanding into a full salon: beautician, masseuse and skin-care expert.

But a successful career wasn't enough. She was lonely, unfulfilled. She wanted to get married. She wanted a husband, a strong and caring man who shared her hopes and dreams.

So why hadn't she found one? Though not beautiful in the true sense of the word, she knew she could hold her own among the female population, having been endowed with clear skin, violet-colored eyes and a cap of black hair.

Her one drawback, she thought, was her breasts. Her stature was slender and petite, and no matter how little she ate, her breasts remained persistently a touch too generous.

Still, some—especially a man—would consider that more of an asset than a deterrent. Maybe the reason she hadn't found the right partner was that she had no interest in casual sex. Sex, for her, was tied to deep feelings. She never did anything halfway, which was why she often got hurt. What she wanted was to give herself fully to one man, who would risk, as she was willing to, the gamble of commitment.

As ludicrous as it seemed now, when she'd been young and naive, she'd often dreamed of Drew declaring his undying love for her and asking her to marry him.

That stroll down fantasy lane had stemmed from a brief encounter one afternoon when snow had covered the ground, a rarity in East Texas. She had gone outside for some reason and had come upon Drew and Peter, who were mauling each other with snowballs. Suddenly a snowball had landed against her right temple. She'd lost her balance and dropped to the ground.

While both boys had run towards her, it was Drew's hand that had reached out to her.

"Sorry," he said, grinning devilishly. "Are you hurt?"

"No," she said, and gave him her hand.

The contact sent a burst of adrenaline through her veins. But when she made the effort to put distance between them, she inadvertently leaned into the strength of Drew's hard frame.

Sparks shot through her. Stepping back, she felt as if her nerve endings had been burned. "I'm...sorry," she murmured.

Drew smiled at her, his eyes twinkling. "No problem. Glad you weren't hurt."

She'd thought of that moment often through the years. That was the first time she'd realized she had a crush on Drew, and wished he'd pay attention to her instead of to Peter.

But that was not to be, and early on, those foolish, girlish hopes had died a natural death.

No, she feared the man of her dreams didn't exist. That was why she took matters into her own hands concerning a child. At thirty-one, her biological clock was ticking, and Ann felt she must race against time.

A child. She was so busy delighting in that wonderful thought, she failed to hear the doorbell until its rings turned so persistent that she couldn't ignore them.

"I'm coming," she called, dashing across the room and swinging open the door.

"Where were you?" Sophie said without preamble.

Ann smiled. "Congratulating myself, actually."

"Oh? Something happen I should know about?"

Sophie skirted past Ann and marched into the living room. "Well, tell me. Don't keep me in suspense."

"I got a call from the agency."

Sophie's eyes lit. "All right!"

They both giggled, then hugged.

They broke apart finally, only to keep their silly grins in place.

"What are you drinking?" Sophie asked.

"Oops, sorry. My manners aren't what they used to be. It's tea. Want a glass?"

"After today, how about two glasses, one for each hand and dashed with a jigger of bourbon?"

Ann chuckled. "Sit down. I'll be right back."

A few minutes later, they sat facing each other from opposite ends of the sofa.

"So what else did the lady say?" Sophie asked.

Ann leaned over and set her empty glass on the coffee table, then explained.

"So, no baby right away, huh?"

Ann released a heartfelt sigh. "Maybe not for another year or two."

"Jeez. That's too damn long to wait."

"I know, but that's the rule, especially when you're a single parent."

"Sounds like they make it near impossible."

"Almost but not quite." Ann laughed. "Remember, I'm 'active.'"

Sophie laughed back. "Whatever you say."

"By the way, what brought you to my doorstep? Not that you aren't welcome anytime," Ann added hastily, "but—"

"You're right. I did stop by for a reason." Sophie's face sobered. "You don't know, do you?"

"Don't know what?"

"John MacMillan died a little while ago."

"Oh, no."

"It was on the six o'clock news, but I see you don't have your TV on."

"And haven't had."

"I knew you'd want to know," Sophie said, draining her glass, then standing up.

Without saying anything, Ann stood also. When she'd learned that John MacMillan had suffered a life-threatening stroke, she hadn't been able to muster much sympathy. She'd always thought of him as a cold, taciturn man who alienated his own family, most of all his son.

Now that she'd learned of his death, her emotions were mixed. On the one hand, she felt sadness—on the other a sense of justice. She knew she shouldn't think ill of the dead, but John MacMillan's insensitive actions had left a deep scar on her heart.

"The town'll be in a tizzy," Sophie commented.

"I'm sure." Ann felt dazed and rubbed her forehead. John MacMillan dead. That didn't seem possible. His presence had lorded over MacMillan for so long, the town wouldn't be the same without him.

"So, are you going to the funeral tomorrow?" Sophie asked.

Ann watched Sophie closely. "If I do, it won't be out of respect for John, that's for sure."

"That's understandable."

"But Mrs. MacMillan was kind and helpful to my mother. Out of respect for her, I feel I should go."

"What about Drew?"

"What about him?"

Sophie shrugged. "You two always got along, didn't you?"

"Why is it that everyone, including you, stares at me when Drew's name is mentioned?" Ann's tone was sharper than she intended, and immediately she regretted the outburst, although Sophie didn't seem to take offense.

Sophie held up her hands, and her lips quivered with the need to smile. "Whoa, I didn't mean anything by that. Really I didn't. It's just that when his name comes up, you seem to tighten up, get an odd look on *your* face."

"Oh, all right. Maybe I do. At one time, I envisioned us waltzing off together into the sunset and living happily ever after."

Sophie laughed outright. "Sounds good to me."

"Well, dreams have a funny way of not coming true. Anyway, I've recovered from the blow, so you needn't worry."

"I believe you." Sophie headed for the door. "If you want me to, I'll go to the funeral with you."

"Fine. See you tomorrow."

Ann twisted the lock behind Sophie, then leaned against the door and breathed deeply. If Drew hadn't already returned to MacMillan, he would definitely do so now. And she was certain to see him.

So what? It wouldn't make any difference to her one way or the other. She was over him, for god's sake.

Though she knew she could never have Drew or even another man like him, she could have a complete and happy life. Her baby would make that happen.

For the first time in a long while, that thought failed to comfort her.

Three

―――

"John MacMillan will be sorely missed by young and old alike...."

The minister's voice droned as he sang the praises of the town's most important citizen. But Ann couldn't bear to listen to the words another minute. She closed her eyes and willed herself to concentrate on something else.

She and Sophie had not attended the funeral inside the largest Baptist church in town. There hadn't been room for all the mourners. Consequently, loudspeakers had been placed outside so the overflow crowd could hear the service.

Ann had opted only to attend the burial ceremony at the cemetery on the outskirts of town.

Now, as she stood beside Sophie, she pinned her eyes on a bumblebee that hovered over a huge wisteria close by. The smell of the flowering vine wafted past Ann's nose. She breathed deeply of its delicate sweetness.

Weather-wise, the day was perfect. No clouds marred the sky, and the temperature hovered around the seventy-degree mark.

The bee flew away, and Ann faced the minister once again. She felt like a hypocrite. But out of respect for Janet MacMillan, she had felt both duty- and conscience-bound to attend.

Because she and Sophie had arrived only minutes before the service began, she hadn't seen the family. She knew, though, that Drew wouldn't be far from his mother's side. Janet MacMillan was in fragile health herself.

While the minister continued to heap praises on John MacMillan, Ann's thoughts centered on Drew. How was he feeling? she wondered. Sad? Numb? Frustrated? Probably all three, she speculated, knowing of the constant battle between father and son.

Only after Sophie nudged her hand did she notice that everyone's head was bowed and that the minister was saying a prayer. Flushing, Ann lowered her head and shut her eyes tightly. She prayed for forgiveness for her fidgeting and her wandering mind. She shouldn't feel guilty, though. John MacMillan had been a tyrant, and nothing anyone could say or do would convince her otherwise.

Relief rushed through Ann as the minister finally said, "Amen."

The crowd dispersed immediately, except for close friends and family members. Ann wanted a word with Janet MacMillan, but she couldn't bring herself to intrude. Anyway, she wasn't sure how she'd be received, considering it was no secret how she felt about John, though she didn't seem to have garnered any condescending stares for her presence.

"Do you want to speak to any of the family?" Sophie asked in a low voice. "If you do, I'll wait in the car."

"No, no, I don't think so." Ann played with a loose strand of hair. "I'll stop by and see Mrs. MacMillan one day next week."

"Ah, there's Maxine," Sophie said, craning her head. "I need to talk to her a minute. I'll see you in a minute."

Ann nodded, then turned and made her way toward her car, which was parked quite a way from the cemetery. She didn't know what made her twist her head at precisely that moment, but she did, and Drew filled her vision.

He stood slightly off to himself, and was leaning stiffly against a tree. Janet, nearby, was surrounded by friends.

Even yards away, Ann could see the changes the years had wrought. He looked older than his twenty-nine years. But he was still handsome, more so, actually, than she remembered.

He had picked up weight, which complemented rather than detracted from his six-foot-plus frame. Another obvious change was his hair. The blond streaks seemed to dominate, maybe because the gray was mingled with them. His dark tan, along with the blue suit that matched his eyes, depicted a larger-than-life macho man with the power to win women's hearts and break men's jaws.

To her dismay, every fiber of her being prickled with awareness. She hated herself for that weakness. A schoolgirl crush was one thing, but to react this way now was totally unacceptable.

As if Drew sensed he was being scrutinized, he swung around. Their eyes connected. Ann was positive he didn't recognize her. His eyes appeared blank, only to then narrow in surprise.

Ann's heartbeat quickened as he uncoiled his frame and narrowed the space between them. She wished she could read his thoughts. But as their eyes continued to hold, she experienced the same jolting shock of emotion she had had that snowy day long ago when he'd lifted her against him.

"Ann? Ann Sinclair? Is that you?"

She reeled under the put-down. How could he not recognize her? Had she changed that much? She thought not. It just proved how little she had meant to him.

Swallowing convulsively, Ann said, "Hello, Drew." She was relieved that her voice sounded natural, even if she trembled inside.

He didn't extend his hand. For that she was grateful. Something told her not to touch him....

His face was sober, and the lines pronounced. Yet the twinkle in his eyes she remembered so well remained—"a twinkle that could charm the birds right out of a tree," her mother used to say.

"It's been a long time," Drew said, angling his head to one side and gazing at her.

"Yes, it has."

"How've you been?"

"Fine. And you?"

"Till now, fine."

His tone was a mixture of sorrow and anger, though his gaze held steady on her, and Ann felt a rush of heat envelop her. Granted, the afternoon was warm, but the flush inside her had nothing to do with the weather. Drew's nearness brought on the attack to her system and made her want to shed the jacket to her suit.

"How's your mother?" she asked awkwardly, unable to bring herself to say she was sorry about his father.

"She's holding up about as well as can be expected. The shock's been doubly hard on her heart, though."

"She's a special lady," Ann said.

"How's Peter?"

Ann's chin lifted. "Do you really care?"

"As a matter of fact, I do."

"Sorry, I didn't mean to be rude."

"Yes, you did."

Ann's sharp comeback died when she saw the smile tug at the corner of his lips.

"Okay, so I did," she said a trifle breathlessly.

She didn't understand the tension that simmered between them. Maybe it was the past rearing its ugly head. More likely, though, it was her reaction to him.

"I should get back to Mother," he said.

"Of course." She paused. "Look, about John—"

His jaw tensed. "I understand, believe me. After the number he did on your family—"

Ann nodded, feeling her throat tighten.

"Maybe I'll see you around," he said finally.

"Maybe."

He stared at her a moment longer, then pivoted on his heel and strode off.

When she joined Sophie in the car, Ann's breath still came in short spurts.

"You aren't leaving today, are you, son?"

A pang of guilt stabbed Drew; his stomach lurched. He bent down and squeezed his mother's cold, limp hand.

"You know better than that, Mamma." His tone was gentle. "Even if I didn't have the estate to settle, I wouldn't leave you."

Janet MacMillan raised watery eyes, the same color as her son's, and smiled. Before her first heart attack, she'd been a strong, lovely woman. While still lovely, with a cap of thick snow-white hair and almost flawless skin, she was far from strong. Her illness had taken its toll. That, combined with the death of her husband, caused Drew grave concern.

"I know you have your own life, and that—" She broke off, her lips trembling.

"Shh, Mamma. Everything's taken care of. I'm not going anywhere, except maybe to Daddy's office."

Unfortunately, his mother had the knack of reading his mind. She knew he hadn't planned to stay in

MacMillan. But he was trapped. Even if his mother didn't need him, MacMillan Investments did.

"Drew," she said softly, her eyes still troubled.

"Shh, you just rest. We'll talk later."

That conversation had taken place a little while ago, after the housefull of well-meaning friends had paid their respects and left.

Now, instead of going straight to the office as planned, Drew stood at the grave site of his father and stared down at the immense number of flowers that covered the fresh dirt.

He wished he felt something besides this pit of emptiness inside. He wanted to cry, but the tears wouldn't come. He felt as though a rock was lodged in his throat. He had been home only one day when his daddy had died. John had been in a coma and hadn't even been aware of his presence.

Drew paused in his thoughts, shielded his eyes from the harsh sunlight, then gazed around. Where earlier the cemetery had been crawling with people, it was now eerily quiet. Only the hum of a small plane above offered any break in the silence.

He looked back at the grave and wished things had been different, wished he could have been close to the man whose life was now a closed chapter. But no one had had that privilege, not even his mother.

John took and never gave. With Drew he'd been the most unbending. He could never accept his son's brash, happy-go-lucky nature, nor his penchant for living dangerously.

From the time Drew had been a mere child, cars were his favorite toys. That never changed. But what galled John the most was Drew's disinterest in joining the family business. On the day he left for college Drew told John he couldn't care less about MacMillan Investments. They'd quarrelled and had barely spoken since.

"It's too late, now, Dad," Drew whispered in the wind. "But for whatever it's worth, I wanted you to love me. Only you never did, did you?"

He stared at the grave a while longer, then grimfaced, he turned and walked to his car.

Only after he drove through the main street of MacMillan did his mood lighten somewhat. Memories both good and bad swept through him, especially the times he and Peter had dragged Main Street when Drew's daddy was out of town. Old Sheriff Becker had been too chicken to tell his old man.

Thinking of Peter made him think of Peter's sister. Good golly, he couldn't believe the Ann Sinclair who used to bug him and Peter was the same as the Ann Sinclair he'd seen earlier.

The change was miraculous. She'd turned into a heart-stopper. When he'd approached her, his breath had caught in his throat. Where once she'd been skinny and shapeless, she was now model thin and shapely.

But her exquisite looks weren't all. Something else about her struck him. Was it that fresh, untouched look that piqued his interest? She didn't appear to be aware of how she affected people.

He wondered what she did in MacMillan? And if she was married? When he realized where his thoughts had taken him, he muttered a curse. What the hell was wrong with him? He never intended to seriously involve himself with any woman again.

He coveted his free time and wanted to spend it on the racetrack. Someday he intended to qualify for the Indy 500. That desire to compete overshadowed his desire for a permanent relationship. Besides, he'd learned how painful love was. He'd learned that from his daddy, and he'd programmed himself not to care.

He simply had not been able to give of himself to the woman he had fancied himself in love with. Time, devotion, love—they had wanted it all. He didn't know how he knew or even what possessed him to think such a thing, but instinctively he knew Ann Sinclair would most certainly demand all of the above. And more.

A bird screeched overhead. The obtrusive sound jerked Drew's thoughts out of that emotional mine field, only to turn once again to his daddy's grave. He suddenly felt drained to the bone for the lost opportunities and the might-have-beens.''

The only way to heal himself was to finish the job here as soon as possible and get the hell back to Houston, to what he knew best. Fast cars and fast women. And not necessarily in that order.

Four

——

Frustration tightened like a band around Drew's gut. He felt completely overwhelmed as he stared at the stack of papers and folders on his daddy's desk, most of which he hadn't even sorted through.

John's personal and company lawyers had just left. Instead of providing Drew with straight answers and firm facts concerning his daddy's assets and liabilities, they had given him the runaround. He sensed their hesitancy didn't stem from negligence but rather from ignorance. John had kept them in the dark about much of his business dealings. The only one who seemed to know anything was the business manager, Timothy Pollard, who was presently, and Drew suspected conveniently, out of town on business.

Drew's lips narrowed until they almost disappeared. As soon as Mr. Timothy Pollard returned, he would have a lot of questions to answer. Until then, Drew knew he'd just have to sift through the papers and try to glean the state of affairs as best he could.

The phone jangled. Still distracted, he lifted the receiver and muttered a terse, "Hello."

"Got another burr under your butt, huh?"

Drew eased back in the chair. "One thing about you, Skip, you cut to the heart of the matter."

"Always. See no reason to pussyfoot around."

Drew laughed. "What's up?"

"When you coming back?"

"Not anytime soon. Dad's affairs are in a mess. He wasn't nearly as efficient as I'd thought."

"Has anything been finalized?"

"The will's being probated. He left everything to Mother, of course, but she's in no condition to oversee it."

"Well, if there's anything I can do on this end, just holler."

"What about papers that need my signature?"

"There's a stack of 'em."

"Fax them to me."

"The Dallas firm is going to give you a reprieve about the property. Their attorney called a little while ago."

"That's good news," Drew replied. "Or at least I hope so. Get all the facts you can about the area, traffic, etcetera."

"Will do."

"I'm planning to drive down the first of next week, for the day at least."

They said their goodbyes. Drew twisted in the chair and stared out the window. The day held the promise of both sunshine and humidity. He longed to be on the racetrack; it was all he could do to stifle the urge. But Janet depended on him, and he couldn't let her down. Nor did he want to. His mother had made life bearable for him through his childhood. She had done everything in her power to protect him from John's emotional abuse.

Thoughts of his mother brought a smile to his lips. She was the epitome of the genteel Southern lady, liked and respected by everyone in town; the outpouring of love and concern had been proof of that.

Suddenly, unbidden and unwanted thoughts of Ann Sinclair sprang to mind. In many ways her demeanor reminded him of his mother's. He'd thought about Ann a lot since he'd seen her at the cemetery a week ago today.

He wondered again why he was so intrigued by her. He couldn't answer that, except to admit her quiet beauty stirred something inside him. That in itself was crazy because he made a point to stay away from women like Ann Sinclair. Her kind were not for one-night stands, and that was all he was interested in.

He expected his women to know the score, sexually and socially. Innocent, unsophisticated women had never appealed to him. Since he'd sworn off commitments and marriage, anything serious made him nervous. *Ann* made him nervous.

Disgruntled with his thoughts, Drew swung around in his chair and decided what he needed was a cup of strong coffee.

Ann placed the receiver back in its cradle and laughed aloud. Another important call. More good news. She couldn't wait to tell Sophie.

Before the call had come, she'd been busy reviewing her ideas for renovating the supply room. If she was going to handle a skin-care line, additional space was a necessity. The room she and Sophie worked in didn't have a spare inch anywhere.

Ann gave her manicurist table the once-over. Satisfied that everything was in order, she looked up. Like her house, her shop was her creation and equally as charming. She seldom patted herself on the back for anything she did. On the contrary, she was far too hard on herself, expected too much.

But today, during the quiet hours before the shop opened, she once again admired her handiwork. One wall was decorated with a patterned wallpaper that enhanced the thick peach carpet on the floor. The remaining walls were painted white, allowing her to splatter them with posters and pictures, in all colors, sizes and shapes, that pertained to her profession.

Two brass-and-glass étagères held various nail and hair products for sale. Positioned throughout the shop were pots filled with live plants and baskets filled with peach potpourri.

Two other rooms completed the shop. One was the pedicure room; the other was the room she hoped to renovate.

If only her personal life were as rich as her professional one, she'd have it made. Ann frowned as she sat back down. Since the funeral, thoughts of Drew MacMillan had haunted her. Seeing and talking to him at the cemetery had shaken her more than she cared to admit. She had forgotten just how good-looking he was. And when he'd looked at her...

She heard the key turn in the lock and waited until Sophie closed the door behind her before she said, "Guess what?"

Sophie dumped her purse beside her station, then said, "You heard?"

"How did you know?"

"I didn't," Sophie replied. "Just a wild guess."

Excitement shone from Ann's eyes. "They're definitely interested. All Natural is sending a rep by to visit with us, to inspect the shop."

"Really!" Sophie's tone reeked with shock and awe. "Really."

Sophie clapped her hands. "Way to go. Their product is so popular and top of the line. How'd you do it? You must've laid the charm on thick."

"Actually, I don't know why they were so receptive. You know, I thought calling them was a long shot, but I had to try."

"Well, the gamble paid off."

"Not yet. We still have to prove that we can sell a bundle of their products. That means we have to advertise like crazy."

"Right," Sophie said. "Starting today, between customers, I'll work on some stuff."

"Me, too," Ann said, looking down at her book. "Uh-oh, I'm afraid that's out for today."

Sophie crossed to her table. "Ditto. My book is nearly full already. If we have many walk-ins, we're going to be in trouble."

"Just the kind of trouble I love," Ann said, then winced as she thought of the two pedicures she had scheduled, along with two sets of nail tips to apply.

"So, I guess it's to work," Sophie mused aloud.

"And none too soon. Here comes Ms. Riley."

The most popular hangout on the square bore the proud name of The Coffee Cup. The sign was so old and faded that for years Drew had expected it to fall and land on someone's head, but to date, it hadn't budged.

The place buzzed. Drew saw a booth in the far corner and slipped into it, but not before several curious stares and nods were thrown his way. A smiling blond waitress took his order. While he waited for his coffee, he peered out the window, willing his mind to stop spinning.

It was then that he heard his name, followed by teeters of laughter. Curious, he buried his head against the cushioned bench and listened. He hadn't noticed who occupied the booth behind him; he hadn't cared. Until now.

More laughter. He waited. The booth was occupied by several women, he decided as two giggled while another spoke in guarded tones.

The waitress chose that moment to bring his coffee.

"Will there be anything else, sir?"

Drew forced a smile. "No, thanks."

She stared at him a moment longer; curiosity burned in her eyes. Much to his relief, she didn't say anything, merely turned and scuttled away.

Immediately, the booth behind him reclaimed his attention.

The women were whispering. Finally one's voice rose slightly above the others. "Did you see him at the funeral?"

"You'd have to be blind if you didn't," another said.

"I know you shouldn't be aware of things like that at a funeral, but he looked absolutely gorgeous."

Another woman laughed. "You won't get an argument out of me. Drew MacMillan can eat crackers in my bed anytime he wants."

Drew smiled. Mmm. So far so good.

"Why, honey, if Sam heard you say that, he'd kill you."

Drew's smile widened. They were getting braver; their volume level had increased. Drew could hear them now without straining. He just hoped no one else could. Yet he couldn't help but be amused at what he was hearing.

"You two are terrible. He looks good all right," a high-pitched voice said. "But I'm still not sure he can perform."

Drew's smile disappeared along with his smug good humor.

"Oh, for heaven's sake, don't believe everything you read."

"Well," one exclaimed, "if he's really impotent..."

Drew recoiled as if he'd been slapped. He'd heard enough. Without bothering to finish his coffee, he threw a couple of bills on the table and stalked toward the door.

A few minutes later, he walked into the kitchen of the MacMillan mansion, fury pounding through his veins.

Rebecca Cribs, the housekeeper who had been with the family since before he was born, stood in front of the sink. The large airy room smelled of fresh-baked bread.

"You're either sick or mad," she said bluntly, her too-large bosom shaking slightly. "Which is it?"

Because of her devotion and long-standing with the family, she took liberties and got away with them. She was fiercely loyal to the family and would defend and protect them at all costs.

"The latter." Drew's voice quivered with suppressed anger.

"I see. Want a cup of coffee?"

"No thanks. How's Mother?"

"God bless her, she's sleeping. I just checked on her."

"Good," Drew said, then fell quiet, struggling to regain control of himself.

"You sure you don't want to tell me what's got you in such a snit?"

Drew couldn't help but smile. "Ah, Becky, my girl, what would we do without you?"

She blushed at the compliment. "Hope you don't have to find out."

Drew's warm humor vanished. "I just came from the coffee shop where I was being discussed."

"Doesn't surprise me none."

"What does that mean?" he asked, an ashy taste in his mouth.

Rebecca stopped what she was doing and faced him. "You know how people talk, especially about your family. It's not ever going to change."

'You've heard the gossip, haven't you?" Drew asked.

"Yes, but I didn't pay no attention to it. Just filthy gibberish, that's all it is."

"Damn!"

"Watch your mouth. Why, your mamma would have a conniption fit if she heard you say that."

"You won't tell on me now, will you?" Drew's tone was cajoling once again.

A smile added wrinkles to Becky's face. "No." She paused. "I bet I know where that nasty tale got started."

Drew tensed. "Where?"

"Polished Choice."

"What the hell is that?"

"A nail shop. You know, where women go for manicures. Ann Sinclair owns it."

Drew felt his breath lock, as if his throat had iced over. "Well, I'll be damned."

"It's just like a beauty shop...."

Drew no longer listened. He crossed to the door and swung it open.

"Where do you think you're going, young man?" Rebecca demanded in a huffed voice. "It's dinner-time."

"Don't worry. I'll eat later. There's something I've got to do."

With that, he strode out the door and closed it firmly behind him.

The remainder of the day passed in a blur. Both Ann and Sophie did indeed book back-to-back appointments. Ann suspected the dance at the country club this weekend contributed to the rush. Also the local foundry had rehired a hundred workers. The local paper had reported that one factory was awarded a government contract.

Whatever the reason, Ann was thrilled. She loved the hustle and bustle that went along with a busy shop. More than that, the increased business meant she could soon begin her expansion.

"I'm outta here," an exhausted Sophie announced at seven o'clock.

"Whew, I won't be far behind," Ann said. "I don't remember when I've been so tired."

Sophie paused at the door. "See ya."

Ann began readying the shop for tomorrow when she heard a knock on the door. A frown puckered her forehead. Who in the world would knock at this hour? Could be anyone who had seen the light still on in the shop, she guessed. Well, she wasn't about to do a manicure at this late hour, not as tired as she was.

She unlocked the door and flung it open. Drew stood on the porch, slouched against the pillar.

Ann felt her mouth go slack before shock rendered her speechless.

Five

Drew barrelled across the threshold, stopped midway in the room, turned and announced, "I'm going to sue the hell out of you."

As calmly as her jerking muscles would allow, Ann eased toward him, a stunned and perplexed look on her face. "Whatever are you talking about?"

He curled his lips into a sneer. "Don't play the innocent with me."

Aghast, Ann stared at him. She stood close enough to him to sense his strength. The cords in his neck stood out. His shoulders, which needed no padding, bunched.

The hint of a beard showed through despite his morning shave. His high cheekbones, along with the crook in his nose, the latter a trophy from his football years, were also more pronounced.

He wore a pair of black jeans, a casual shirt and boots. And though he appeared calm, Ann knew better. He was madder than hell, which made him that much more sinfully attractive.

"Stalling isn't going to do you any good."

Ann manufactured a brave, cool smile. "I still don't know what you're talking about. You come in here like something wild, and start flinging around accusations that—"

"Save it," he said rudely.

Ann jutted her chin and clenched her fists until her knuckles felt as if they would pop through her skin. But that didn't halt his bold, appraising gaze. It toured her hidden curves with insolent deliberation. The deep brilliance of his eyes, which she remembered from youth, had lost none of their disturbing sensuality.

She lowered her head and concentrated on removing a thread that clung to her slacks. When crossed, Drew's easygoing personality ceased to exist. Apparently she had crossed him in some way, or at least he thought she had. He liked his own way, she thought, remembering moments when he and Peter would have a heated disagreement. He would pour on the charm one minute, only to turn meaner than a junkyard dog the next.

Despite that, Ann gave in to the forbidden temptation of seeing how far she could push him. She lifted her chin defiantly. "This is *my* property, and I could demand that you leave."

"Wouldn't do you any good," he said with arrogant self-assurance.

Ann saw red. Just who did he think he was? She grappled to speak, but choking anger made it impossible.

"Somehow, I thought you were different." He snorted. "But you're not. You're just like all the rest of the women I know. You just can't control your tongue."

"Control my tongue!" Ann's voice matched her body temperature. "For heaven's sake, stop talking in riddles."

"Nasty rumors." He loomed over her. "Does that ring a bell?"

"You're way off base," she flung back.

He smiled, but it didn't last. "You can stand here and tell me that my name *wasn't* discussed in your shop?"

The heat drained from her face. Ah, so that was what this was all about. The society-page article and its consequences were rearing its ugly head. Again. And both times involved her.

"Look," she finally said with a shudder, "I won't deny you were talked about, but—"

"But what?"

"Please, just let me finish, okay?"

"I'm listening."

"If there was anything said about you outside these walls, it didn't come from me. As far as what others say—well, I can't be responsible."

"Do you have any idea how it feels to overhear that kind of garbage?"

"Don't you think you're being a tad dramatic?" she asked lightly, trying to put his conversation in perspective. "Surely you have better things to do than worry about what people say about you?"

He broke contact with her eyes. "Some things yes, others no."

She'd have to concede he was right. When a man's sexuality was questioned, he did tend to lose his objectivity. Still, she wasn't about to take the blame for some scatterbrained women who had discussed him with such zest. She had warned them to keep their mouths shut. If only she'd made that warning stronger.

"So, what did you contribute to the conversation?"

Ann blinked in confusion. "What?"

"You heard me."

He was deliberately baiting her, and she knew it. Well, she wasn't about to be a party any longer to the need to have his ego massaged. True, he'd just lost his daddy and was going through a tough time. But that didn't give him the right to take his frustration out on her.

She turned and walked to the window, unable to think with him so close. The late-evening sunlight spilled into the room and created weird designs across the carpet.

Finally, Ann faced him again and said with saccharine sweetness, "All right, if I've caused you to suffer unduly, I apologize."

Suddenly tired of the whole fiasco, Ann deliberately yawned, then raised her arms and stretched, unaware that her breasts teased the thin material of her blouse, leaving no doubt as to their generous fullness.

The sharp intake of Drew's breath made her realize what she had done. The gaze that had searched her face now moved to her breasts. And lingered.

The atmosphere in the room was charged.

Desperate to diffuse it, Ann began, "I think—"

"Prove it?" His voice was gruff.

"Excuse me?"

"Prove it?"

"How?" she asked with uncomfortably hot cheeks.

Drew hesitated only a second. "Cook dinner for me."

What was he doing? Playing another silly game? Daring her? A little of both, she guessed. But why? He had gotten what he'd come for—an apology, albeit a backhanded one.

"Say tomorrow night?" His eyes probed. "At eight?"

She felt as if she were on a roller coaster. Her stomach heaved, and she had trouble catching her breath. Sexual stares and innuendos weren't totally foreign to her. She'd received her fair share. But never with the same intensity that Drew looked at her now. It seemed as if he could see through her clothes, to her naked flesh.

She moistened her lips with her tongue. "Tomorrow night," she croaked. "At eight."

His eyes focused on her face, then he turned and sauntered out the door.

If Ann hadn't been leaning against the windowsill, she would have collapsed. What on earth had come over her? Involving herself with the likes of Drew MacMillan was tantamount to stepping on a lighted firecracker; it could only burn her. It was but a matter of time until he returned to Houston for good.

Even so, she found she couldn't stymie the dangerous excitement that bubbled inside her. If nothing else, the evening would be interesting.

"How far back did you want them?"

Drew stared at his daddy's secretary, Rose, with unseeing eyes. His thoughts were splintered in so many different directions that he couldn't concentrate on any one thing for long.

"The financial records, sir? How far back?"

"Sorry, Rose," Drew said, forcing himself to smile at her. She was a plain woman, in her early fifties, whose loyalty to his father had probably bordered on fear.

Now, as she waited patiently for his answer, the lines around her mouth seemed to have intensified. Her fear now stemmed from worry over losing her job. Well, she was right. The whole lot of employees had better worry. The company's finances and holdings should have been in better shape than they were. He aimed to find out why they weren't.

"Five years back. And Rose, what's the word on Tim Pollard?"

The company's business manager was still missing. Drew felt sure he was key to part of this mess.

"Actually, he did call before you got here." Rose paused.

"Go on," Drew prompted with uncharacteristic patience.

"He's . . . back in town."

"Why wasn't I told?"

"He said he'd contracted some kind of contagious virus and couldn't come back to the office for at least another week."

"How convenient," Drew said sarcastically.

Rose flushed. "Shall I call him back and—"

Drew cut her off. "No, don't bother."

Once she had gone, Drew transferred his attention back to the stack of papers in front of him. How much longer could he jockey his thoughts between here and Houston? With each day that passed, it became more difficult. His car dealerships alone needed his undivided attention. Now he was seeped in a mess far beyond his imagination. To think that his daddy, who was supposed to have been the consummate businessman, could have let his business deteriorate to such an extent was untenable.

Lamenting over spilled milk wasn't the answer, Drew reminded himself sharply, but tackling the ledger was.

Instead of figures, however, Ann's face swam before his eyes. He slammed the folder shut, closed his eyes and cradled his forehead in his hands.

Insane! Or maybe stupid. He still couldn't believe he'd asked Ann to cook him dinner. Of all the dense things he could have done or said, that one topped the list.

He'd made his first mistake by going to her shop. But dammit, his pride had been at stake. His manhood. And still was. God, what were people thinking about him? What were they saying? Usually he couldn't care less what people thought of him. They could go to hell if they didn't like what he did or said. He hadn't even let his old man intimidate him.

But the idea that someone might believe that rubbish and think that he was impotent—

A renewed wave of disgust rushed through him. What did Ann think?

"Knock it off, MacMillan."

But nothing short of a brain transplant could stop him from thinking about Ann. Erotic thoughts, at that. When she'd lifted her arms, and he'd seen those burgeoning breasts...

In that heated moment when their eyes had met, everything had changed. Something had given way inside him.

That insane feeling hadn't resulted from the sexual fireworks between them. That was part of it, all right. He wouldn't deny that. But the way she'd stood up to him after he'd stormed into her shop like a caged tiger turned loose was to her credit. She'd thrust out her chin and faced him squarely.

No, he couldn't blame sex alone for the turbulence raging inside him. It went deeper, scaring the hell out of him.

Six

"I'll have to say that was one of the best, if not the best, meals I've ever eaten." Drew smiled lopsidedly as he lowered himself next to her on the couch, all the while rubbing his stomach.

Ann felt herself blush, even though she knew his compliment was due to part baloney and part charm. Nevertheless, it pleased her. She would hate to think she'd spent hours in the kitchen for nothing.

"I'm glad you enjoyed it," she said, embarrassed by the breathless tremor in her voice.

But then it had been there ever since he'd rung the doorbell and she'd let him in. She hadn't known what to expect from herself or from him. All afternoon she'd been in a tizzy, cleaning the house, cooking, making sure everything was perfect. Thank heavens, business had been slow at the shop, which had allowed her to leave at noon.

Once she'd finished the other chores, she'd started on preparing herself. She'd soaked in a hot bubble bath, washed and dried her hair and had taken extra pains with her makeup. She'd pondered what to wear, had finally chosen a pair of red silk slacks and matching capped-sleeved blouse. The outfit had been an indulgent splurge, and she knew she looked her best in it.

She'd tried then to put the evening in perspective, reminding herself that he wanted nothing from her except a meal. When the evening ended, he would walk out the door and that would be it.

But when he'd grinned at her from across the threshold, her bones had turned to rubber.

"Hi," he'd said.

She didn't move, but managed to say, "Hi."

He cocked his head. "Are we dining outside?"

"No, of course not," she said, and shook her head.

He laughed. "Well, then, don't you think you'd better ask me in?"

Ann felt her cheeks turn scarlet before she stepped aside to let him enter. "Sorry."

"God, it smells like heaven in here," he said, inhaling deeply.

"It's homemade bread."

"You made it?"

She nodded and joined him in the middle of the living room.

"I didn't know anyone did that anymore."

"I don't very often."

A strand of sandy hair fell over his brow. Her finger itched to brush it back. Instead, she moved slightly, out of harm's way.

"Is dinner ready?"

"I take it you're hungry."

An awareness passed between them, holding them both motionless.

Drew cleared his throat. "I haven't eaten all day."

"It's . . . it's ready when you are."

They'd gone straight to the brightly decorated table where he'd consumed two huge helpings of chicken, salad and homemade bread. The conversation had remained light and impersonal. Ann had been too nervous to eat much, but had enjoyed watching him make the most of the meal.

To her relief, there had been few awkward moments. Those had come only after she would laugh at something outlandish he'd said. She'd catch him watching her with a strange expression in his eyes, one that not only disconcerted her but made her feel warm all over.

Now, as she watched him continue to massage his stomach, his legs sprawled before him, she couldn't seem to stop herself from staring.

He had on a pair of jeans and a yellow shirt that magnified his blue eyes and dark tan. She thought of the hard-tone muscles under his clothes and swallowed, feeling the way she had years ago when she had a crush on him. But that was absurd. When he left, her heart would settle along with the rest of her and she'd see him for what she knew he was: an eternal ladies' man who had no intention of making a commitment.

"Not only can you cook, but your tea is the best." He proceeded to drain his glass.

She moved to get up and refill it.

He held up his hand and broadened his smile. "Keep your seat. I'll do it." He then took her glass from her.

"You won't hear an argument out of me." Ann eased back on the couch. "You sure you wouldn't rather have a beer?"

"Nope. When I leave here, I'm going back to the office to do some paperwork."

"Ah, so you need a clear head?"

"Right," he said with a disarming grin.

If he didn't stop grinning at her like that, she wasn't sure she could be held responsible for her actions. While he ambled into the kitchen, Ann felt her breath released from her tightened throat. She went limp as a rag doll. God, she had to get hold of her frayed emotions....

She heard his footsteps and forced a cool smile onto her lips. But the minute he came into view, that smile faltered. The closer he came, the louder her nagging conscience: *you're lying to yourself.* His physical power dominated the room, shrinking its size. He wouldn't be able to simply walk out of her life without repercussions, she thought with a sinking heart.

Her blood pressure wasn't up because of fear of further confrontation but because he was here with her.

He returned to his seat beside her on the couch, then held out her glass. "Don't say I didn't ever do anything for you."

Later, Ann suspected the accidental touch hadn't been part of the game plan, but it happened, nevertheless. The soft, but exquisite graze of fingers sent a current through her entire body.

Drew seemed to feel it, too. He flinched visibly, then changed the subject.

"What do you hear from Peter these days?"

Ann's face clouded. "Not anything, actually."

"Does that bother you?"

"Yes and no," she said with a sigh.

"Is it true that he's been in trouble with the law?"

"Yes." Bitterness colored her tone. "I hear from him when he needs something."

"That's a damn shame. He had...has so much potential."

"True. But Mamma always said he didn't have a backbone."

"I tried to help, you know."

"I know, but he resented it." Ann looked at her hands. "I keep hoping, praying, that one of these days he'll straighten up."

"Maybe he will," Drew said, his eyes on her.

A short silence ensued.

"Look, the evening was great, but I've got to go." He sounded desperate, yet he made no move to get up.

"So, I'm vindicated?" Ann said, returning his stare.

His lips tightened. "Go ahead and say it."

"What?" she asked, feigning innocence.

He grinned sheepishly. "That I acted like the world's biggest jackass."

"I didn't say that."

"But you thought it."

"Well..."

He chuckled. "God, I can't believe I came charging into your shop blaming you. But when Becky told me those quacking biddies had heard it at your place, I lost it."

"Well, in defense of yourself, you'd had a week from hell. John dying, worry over your mother, then hearing someone accuse you of being im..." Her voice faltered, and she couldn't go on.

"*Impotent.* That's the word," he said with a teasing glint in his eyes.

She flushed, but couldn't control her tongue. "Only you're not..." Again her voice faltered.

"I may be a lot of things. But that I'm not." His eyes bored into hers.

"I'm...glad."

He laughed at her response. "Me, too."

She liked to hear him laugh, even if it was at her expense. It originated in his chest and ended in his eyes, lightening them even more.

She liked everything about this man—his deep, husky voice, the way his hair begged for a trim, the way he smelled....

But he wasn't interested in her.

Or so she told herself, until the laughter stopped and his eyes met hers. Something sizzled between them, something alive and vital. An ache began deep inside her, and her nipples throbbed. But he never looked at her breasts. He never got the chance.

She leapt to her feet and walked to the middle of the room.

He cleared his throat. "Uh, tell me what you do?"

She swung around. "Do?"

"Yeah, you know. Your work."

"Oh." She relaxed. "I turn ugly nails into beautiful ones."

He shook his head. "And you actually make a living doing that?"

"A good one, too. And I have plans to make it even better."

"How?"

She explained about her expansion plans.

"Sounds like you know what you're doing."

"What about you?"

He shrugged. "I guess you could say I live to race."

"I can see you haven't changed."

"Nope. Cars are in my blood."

"Bet you didn't think you'd be selling them for a living, though?"

"Hell, no. I figured in the end, my old man would haul me back to the ranch, so to speak, and put me to work in the lumber mill."

"Only he didn't."

"It wasn't because he didn't want to, believe me. When I told him I had no intention of taking over the family business, he went berserk. Anyway, this college buddy of mine was a car nut like me and wanted to own his own business—used cars, that is. He needed some bucks. So I took my grandmother's trust fund and went in with him. Later he bought me out, and I bought a new car business."

"And now your success enables you to play?"

"If you call racing a game, then I guess it does."

"So when do you race again?"

His features dimmed. "Not anytime soon, not with the mess Dad's estate's in."

"I'm sorry," Ann said for lack of anything better to say.

"Yeah, me, too." He stood abruptly. "Speaking of work. If I don't get outta here, it's never going to get done."

She walked him to the door. Once there, they faced each other. Suddenly there was nothing to say. Throughout the evening, conversation had flowed. But now it seemed to dry up.

"Drew?"

For an interminably long moment they stared at each other.

Drew reached for her, pulled her hard against him. Stillness. Nothing but their breathing and the sound of crickets chirping outside. She felt that incredible heat building inside her again.

Her lips parted, only to be crushed beneath his. It was as if her touch had set him on fire. His tongue invaded her mouth—hot and wet and fierce.

Ann locked her hands around his neck, sinking her fingers into his hair even as she feared his energy might consume her. Still, she clung to him. Her breasts shook with raging emotion. She felt a heavy sensation in her thighs.

The taste of lust was on his lips. He devoured her mouth as if he were no longer in control of himself.

He pulled away then, struggling for breath, and lifted his head to suck air deep into his lungs.

Ann heard the loud thump of her heart. Or was it his?

"Damn," he muttered.

Ann turned away and closed her eyes. Tears of shame and mortification seeped out and down her cheeks. How could she have lost control so easily?

"Look, I'll be in touch," he said, his voice sounding like rough sandpaper.

"All right," she managed to get out. But she couldn't bring herself to look at him again.

A few seconds later, she was alone.

Seven

Drew scrutinized Tim Pollard. With black hair, round face, thick glasses and slightly oversize ears, he reminded Drew of an owl.

But how Pollard looked wasn't the issue; his stupidity was. How Pollard thought he could continue to take money out of the MacMillan till and not get caught went beyond Drew's reasoning.

Besides examining the ledgers, Drew had checked out Pollard personally, certain he'd find a change in Pollard's life-style. He'd turned up zilch, except for one thing. Pollard had a girlfriend. The pillar of the local church fooled around on his wife with a teller at the bank.

A niggling in the back of Drew's mind told him Pollard's liaison with the teller meant something. But

Pollard's bank account hadn't shown anything. The balance had fluctuated very little, if any, over the past few years. He'd just have to keep digging.

Still, Pollard was a hard nut to crack. Drew had called him into the office thirty minutes ago and had been questioning him since.

But the business manager gave no sign that he was intimidated in the least, except that he seemed to have a penchant for running his finger around his collar as if he were choking to death.

"I have been a valuable asset to Mr. MacMillan," Tim said primly, bridging the lengthy silence. "And I don't appreciate your insinuations."

"Well, I don't like what the company's bank account insinuates, either." Drew's tone, while calm, was cold and unyielding.

Tim flushed and again dug his finger between his neck and collar. "I assure you the books are in perfect order. Have them checked."

"I intend to, Mr. Pollard."

When Pollard walked out of his office a few minutes later, Drew cursed silently and rubbed his tired eyes. What a mess. What a bloody mess. He was not an accountant and didn't profess to know the finer points of that trade. However, his gut told him the MacMillan Investments should be showing more of a profit. As he'd told Pollard, the books simply didn't add up.

He knew who could help him, if anyone could. His own accountant in Houston. That was a start anyway. Along with the ledgers, he'd box the invoices, statement and daily cash receipts that Pollard had been responsible for and take them with him.

Drew rubbed his eyes again and tried to ignore the burning sensation behind them. He'd been awake half the night. His mother had had another "incident" with her heart. She'd refused at first to go to the hospital, saying that if she were going to die, she preferred to do so in her own bed. He'd argued, of course, and in the end had won. He had remained by her side at the hospital all night and because her condition had greatly improved this morning, he'd brought her home.

Becky had assured him that she would call him if there was the slightest change in his mother's condition. But nothing could put his mind at ease. It was on a collision course. *He* was on a collision course.

Ann Sinclair was the culprit.

He couldn't shake her from his thoughts. He couldn't get that kiss off his mind. It had been five days since he'd darted out of her house like a scared teenager on his first date. But her response to him had both excited and shocked him. Cool on the outside... hot on the inside.

He still hadn't been able to justify his actions or lay the entire episode to rest. So what if he'd kissed her and she'd kissed him back? Happened with women all the time. No big deal. But it was a big deal. He hadn't wanted to stop there.

When she'd trembled in his arms, and when she'd stirred against him, he'd felt the vibrations clear down to his toes. His heart had raced, and the banked fire in his gut had roared to life.

And her mouth. It had been waiting for him—hot, moist, hungry. The burning inside him had almost leapt out of control. His baser instinct had been to lower her to the carpet, free her breasts and suck those taunting nipples that had bored holes in his chest. But he hadn't wanted to stop there. He'd wanted to jerk off her pants and bury himself inside her hot flesh.

Suddenly he couldn't breathe. Something crushed his chest. Fear? Gut-deep fear, that was what it was. He didn't want to get involved, for god's sake. What was more, he wasn't about to get involved.

He was determined to stay the hell away from her. He already had enough problems. He didn't need extra baggage.

Yeah, that was the answer. But could he do it? He closed his eyes and contemplated the whole damn problem. Finally he came to a decision. Only problem was, he didn't like it.

Disgusted, Drew slammed his hand against the desk.

Raising a Responsible Child by Dr. Don Dinkmeyer. Ann had purchased the book before coming home from the local bookstore.

She eyed the book, even lifted it to her chest, as she'd done several times since she'd gotten home from work. She'd eaten a bite, showered, then slipped into her gown.

She'd been so tired and the bed had looked so inviting, she'd plopped down and hadn't budged.

That had been hours ago. But she hadn't slept nor had she read the book with any real interest.

"Drew," she whispered aloud, despising the twist that darted through her.

During work hours, she did just fine. She kept thoughts of him repressed because they were too painful. But at night, she wasn't as lucky. She thought about her wanton behavior, and she wanted to die.

Ann leaned over and switched off the lamp. She lay against the pillows in the darkness, and listened to the pounding of her heart—and felt her cheeks blaze.

She'd practically swooned at his feet, as though she'd been starved for a man. She hadn't been, of course. Yet when his tongue had tangled with hers, wet and frisky, common sense had deserted her. She had to admit that.

And Drew MacMillan, of all people. A renegade, a lady's man, a velvet-tongued charmer. He was everything she *didn't want* in a man, in the father of her child.

She bolted out of bed and crossed to the window. After opening the miniblinds, she peered outside. A light rain caressed the windowpane. The streets would be as slippery as black glass.

The way Drew drove, she hoped he'd stay off of them. Stop it! Stop thinking about him, she told herself. But as before, her mind and heart seemed determined to take that dangerous turn. No rest for the weary, she told herself.

For years she had kept her personal life on a tight rein, buried her desires. How could she let Drew change that? How could she have veered out of control so easily? So quickly? Well, she wouldn't do it again. Drew MacMillan was off-limits.

Holding on to that comforting thought, she padded back to bed, lay down and jerked the covers over her head.

"Oh, Ann, they look absolutely gorgeous."

Pleased with the praise, Ann smiled. "You really think so?"

"Oh, gosh, yes," Kay Townsend responded. She held out all ten fingers and admired the set of acrylic nails, painted a stunning pink. Ann had adhered the false nails to Kay's natural ones.

"But the question is, can you fix hair with those claws?" Ann asked.

"Like a charm."

"I'm going to hold you to that promise," Ann said, a teasing warmth in her voice.

She had only that morning hired Kay as the first of many beauticians for Polished Choice, or so she hoped. After hours, she had interviewed several girls from MacMillan who were fresh out of beauty school as well as several from nearby towns. She'd wanted to make sure she found just the right person. Her and Sophie's relationship was such that a third person had to fit in, had to have the same work habits and share the same level of enthusiasm.

Though tall and rather gangly, Kay had a style all her own that began with a mop of long blond hair that Ann guessed was not altogether out of a bottle. More importantly, Kay had an infectious smile and gift of gab that was necessary to make a success of her profession.

"When do you think I'll be able to start?" Kay asked.

Ann also rose, then hesitated. "I'm afraid I can't answer that. The carpenter has promised he would work on Sundays and Mondays while the shop's closed. I figure he should be through in about two weeks." She paused with a grimace. "But you know how that is. I've never had much luck with carpenters sticking to their word."

"We can always hope."

Kay walked toward the empty room that was soon to be her new workplace. Ann followed. They stood just inside the doorway.

"I've dreamed of this time for two years," Ann said, her voice shaky. "And now that it's about to become a reality, I'm both scared and excited."

Kay smiled. "Ah, don't be scared, just be excited. Everything's going to be hunky-dory. You wait and see. She faced Ann without the smile. "Are you sure you don't want to move your station in here?"

"Heavens no," Ann exclaimed. "Anyway, you're not going to be alone."

"I'm not?"

Ann chuckled. "Well, there won't be another body." She paused. "But hopefully, All Natural skin-care products will share your space."

"Really?"

"I'm keeping my fingers crossed. A rep is due soon to look us over."

"Wow. 'All Natural.' I'm impressed."

"Don't be—because I might not pull it off. I'm afraid they might demand a higher volume than we can produce. But it doesn't cost anything to dream."

"Do you mind if I stop by and monitor the progress?" Kay asked, inching toward the front door.

"I'll be disappointed if you don't."

Once Ann was alone, she made the shop ready for the day. Sophie was due any minute, and so was her first customer, Mabel. And if Mabel so much as mentioned Drew, Ann was going to pop her in the chops.

Now, wasn't that a delightful thought. Ann flipped the sign on the door and chuckled aloud.

The hours that followed passed quickly, despite the fact that Ann wasn't booked solid nor was Sophie. Still, Ann had a zillion things to do before five o'clock, when she had a pedicure scheduled.

"Sophie, I'll be in the pedicure room. Agnes Gaits will be in shortly."

"Well, I'm outta here, okay?"

"All right. See you in the morning."

Despite her unsettled night, Ann didn't feel tired. Nervous energy propelled her, but she didn't care. As long as she could work without forbidden thoughts of Drew interrupting, she was content.

She even hummed a tune while retrieving the foot-massaging machine from the supply closet. The buzzer on the door sounded.

"Come on back. I'm setting up."

"For what?"

Panic flared inside Ann like a fever. She would have known that gravelly sounding voice anywhere. Every nerve prickled with awareness. Darn her traitorous body. *Darn him!*

She spun around.

The expression in his eyes was unreadable.

"How'd you get in here?" she demanded in a mangled voice. She clutched the massager to her chest as if it were protection for her quaking insides.

He grinned that lazy grin of his. "Walked in, actually."

"Funny," she said, mustering a weak, wobbly smile, determined to show him she was in charge.

"What'cha doing?"

Eight

Drew's tone, lazy as his lopsided grin, brought to life the same "something" she'd felt when his tongue had stormed her mouth. She completely forget his question as she lifted rounded eyes to his.

His grin faded, and his eyes narrowed.

Neither one said a word, neither moved, as they both remembered the last time they were together.

Drew shifted, then cleared his throat, though he never took his eyes off of her.

Her cheeks on fire, Ann bent down, determined to hide her embarrassment. She placed the massager on the floor and made a big deal out of plugging it in.

Why was he here? she ranted silently. She figured he didn't want to see her any more than she wanted to see him. *Liar!* You want to see him, only you know in the end you'll be the one that gets hurt.

Why didn't he stop tormenting her and leave her alone? He was here now and apparently had no intention of leaving. So she'd just have to make the best of an impossible situation and take charge.

"Mind explaining what you're going to do with that?" he asked.

Ann straightened. "It's a foot massager."

"Whatever you say."

In spite of herself, Ann smiled. "Hey, don't knock it. Next to acrylic nails, it's my biggest money-maker."

He still looked blank but made an attempt to fake it. "Uh, how so?"

Ann's smile strengthened. She felt at an advantage for the first time since his surprise visit. "This is used for pedicures," she said with confidence.

"And that is?"

"Oh, come on. You're putting me on. Surely you know what a pedicure is. Anyway," she went on, indulging herself and him, "pedicures are manicures of the feet. I do everything to feet that I do to hands."

"What's this gizmo?" Drew pushed away from the doorjamb and moseyed toward a sturdy white wooden bench that resembled an animal, a giraffe to be exact. He touched it while his gaze met hers. His mouth twitched with amusement. "This is strange, you'll have to admit."

"This gizmo, as you call it, is where I sit."

He crossed his arms, spread his legs slightly and rocked on his heels. He had on jeans, as usual, and a green knit shirt that stretched across his muscled chest.

God, but he was good-looking, Ann thought, her mouth going dry as cotton.

"And they sit in that chair in front?"

"Er...right," Ann said, and collected her scattered senses. "And after I cut or file the nails, remove the excess skin from their heels, etcetera, they soak their feet, then dip them in hot, scented wax. The polish comes next."

"So some lucky woman's about to get the works, huh?"

"Who said it was a woman?"

Drew looked stunned. "You mean it's a man?"

His expression was priceless. Ann chuckled. "Would that be so terrible?"

"You mean you'd actually do all this to men's stinking feet?"

She laughed out loud this time. "Of course. Their feet don't smell any worse than some women's."

"I don't give a damn. A man shouldn't get his feet 'done.'" He paused. "I wouldn't be caught dead in that chair."

"Never say never," she responded airily.

He eyed the "gizmo" with distaste. "In this case, never is never."

"If it'll put your mind at rest," she said with false sweetness, "my client today is a woman. I just wanted to get your reaction."

"Well, you got it."

A twinkle appeared in Ann's eyes. "However, I do have several male clients."

Drew snorted.

Ann heard the buzzer again. "Look, my lady's here." She paused. "Was there...er...something you wanted?" she forced herself to ask.

"Yeah, would you like to go with me to Houston tomorrow?"

"Why?" she asked, her tone wary.

His gaze didn't waver. "No reason, except I'd like the company."

Ann's mind raced. "Well, I..."

"If I promise to keep my hands to myself, will you come?"

A short silence.

"All right, I'll go," she whispered. So much for good intentions, she thought, her heart hammering wildly.

"Good. I'll pick you up about eight."

"So what do you think?"

Ann picked up on the "little boy" eagerness in his tone, despite his efforts to appear nonchalant. She smiled and gave in to the urge to rattle him a bit. "I think exactly what you thought I'd think."

He frowned. "What the hell kind of answer is that?"

She laughed. "Oh, all right, it's a showplace. Now, are you satisfied?"

"Completely," he said with his usual arrogance.

Ann rolled her eyes, then surveyed the surroundings with critical intent. She could find nothing to criticize.

They had left MacMillan around eight o'clock. When Drew had arrived at her house, she'd had butterflies the size of elephants in her stomach. She hadn't as yet come to grips with the idea that she had agreed to this lark. She despised the effect he had on her; his presence made it impossible for her to remain strong. How would she handle being closed up in the car with him for two hours? What would they talk about?

She needn't have worried. He'd striven to put her at ease. After pleasantries had been exchanged, he'd slipped in a cassette of Cher's latest album and they'd listened to it. The strains from the Jag's elaborate stereo system were like none she'd ever heard.

The tension, however, had remained. She was aware of every move he made, no matter how small or insignificant. So when he'd let her out at Town and Country Mall to shop, relief had washed through her.

He'd come after her only thirty minutes ago. Now, they were at his Jaguar dealership.

"I wanted everything to be just right," Drew said close to her ear, "so Mother had a friend whose daughter was an interior decorator." He waved his hand. "The showroom is her handiwork."

In more ways than one, Ann thought cattily. Jealousy, wild and fierce, rushed through her. With an abrupt twist of her head, she forced herself to take in the details that surrounded her.

The showroom floor, though tastefully decorated with plush gold carpeting, huge decorator buckets filled with live plants, and paintings positioned on the paneled walls, actually paled in comparison to the automobiles.

To the side of the main showroom were small offices. A long hall, she suspected, led to Drew's office and the service department beyond. But again, it was the automobiles themselves that made the showroom come to life, added to the refinement.

Ann tried not to show her awe as she inspected the sleek machinery in front of her. She placed her hand on the side of the cranberry-colored Jag and felt as if she were stroking velvet.

"Nice, isn't it?" Drew said from close behind her.

Chill bumps danced across her skin. Without looking at him, she stepped closer to the car. "That's hardly the word."

"Want to sit inside?"

He opened the door and released the new-car scent. Ann inhaled deeply. "It even smells expensive."

"It's supposed to."

She angled her head to one side and peered at him. "How much does one of these jewels sell for?"

"This one, the XJ6 4.0, goes for thirty-three, four."

Ann gulped. "As in dollars?"

His lips twitched. "Good ole American hard, cold cash."

"What about the one over there?" She nodded toward the steel-blue one that revolved under a spotlight.

"That little beauty goes for over forty."

"It must be nice, is all I can say."

Before Drew could respond, a man walked up. Drew introduced him as Skip Howard. They talked for a moment, then Drew turned to Ann. "I need to sign some papers."

"No problem."

"You'll be all right?"

That intimate look again. Her blood pressure shot up, and she ran her tongue over her lips. "Of course."

His eyes delved into hers a second longer. "I won't be long."

He wasn't. Thirty minutes later, they left the dealership and were once again closeted in the car. Ann shifted sideways so that she could study his profile. Instead, her eyes fell to his hands, and she watched as they effortlessly guided the steering wheel. Skill and energy seemed to flow from each finger. She wondered what those fingers would feel like caressing her naked flesh, exploring her body's hidden secrets.

"So what did you do while I was at the mall?" she asked suddenly, desperately, and was rewarded that she had successfully covered the cracks in her voice.

Drew turned and gave her a quick look, his eyes crinkled at the corners. "Met with my accountant."

"Mmm, sounds interesting."

He laughed, then eased a hand off the steering wheel and rested it on his thigh, a thigh that appeared rock hard underneath his casual slacks. "No, it doesn't. It sounds boring as hell."

His laughter added another dimension to the camaraderie they found themselves sharing. Ann angled her head. "Was it? Boring as hell, I mean?"

"No, in light of the fact that I'm trying to nail Pollard's butt."

"Tim Pollard?"

"One in the same."

"Whatever for?" Ann stared at him in amazement. "Why he's one of the pillars of the community. And if I'm not mistaken, a good friend of your family's."

"You're right. My mother went to school with him and thought of him as a close friend. No 'hanky-panky,' mind you, just good friends."

"And isn't he a deacon at church?"

"Front row, amen corner." Drew's voice was thick with sarcasm.

"He must've done something terrible for you to turn on him like this."

"If my suspicions prove correct, you bet he has."

"I can't imagine. Why, he looks like he'd be too scared to do anything wrong." Tim Pollard's face sprang to mind, and she shook her head. She'd always thought of him as a benign being. "Are you sure you're not mistaken?"

"I shouldn't be telling you this, but I think he's been taking money from the till."

"You're kidding?"

Drew shot her a sharp glance. "Would I kid about something like that?"

"No, no you wouldn't."

"He's embezzling, pure and simple."

"But how? How could he get by your daddy? I can't imagine a man like John MacMillan not taking care of his business."

"Nor can I."

"Despite all his other faults," Ann said bluntly, "I'd always admired his business savvy."

"Apparently, he had total confidence in Tim Pollard."

Ann let out a pent-up breath. "I'm here to tell you I'm shocked."

"How the hell do you think I feel? I thought everything would be in great shape, that it'd be a breeze to settle his estate. Then, as soon as Mother stabilized, I'd head back for the bright lights."

Her life would be much simpler if he had, Ann thought. "Only it hasn't worked out that way," she said.

"Not hardly. I guess Dad just got complacent and didn't see any reason to question Pollard. I don't know. Anyway, today I took a ton of stuff to my accountant for him to go through. Maybe he can confirm what I suspect."

"What are you going to do if you find out it's true?"

Drew laughed without humor. "Have the sonofabitch arrested, that's what."

Ann had no doubt he would, thinking again how easygoing he was until crossed. Then there was hell to pay. She shivered.

"What's wrong?" Drew asked.

She forced a smile. "Nothing."

"Surely you don't think I should just slap his hand and let him off the hook?"

Ann chose her words carefully. "No. It's…just that it'll be an awful scandal. I was thinking about his wife and two children."

A muscle tightened in Drew's cheek. "He should've thought about them before he got greedy."

"I know," Ann replied, her tone still troubled.

He looked at her strangely for a moment. "So what about you?" he asked, changing the subject. "What did you accomplish?"

"Shopped."

"For clothes?"

"Uh-huh."

His eyes slowly looked over her. It could have been her imagination, of course, but she was certain they lingered on her breasts as he said, "What are you, a size four?"

She saw the heat in his eyes and could hardly get her breath. "A two, except for—" She broke off, appalled at her near slip of the tongue, at what she was about to admit.

"Your breasts," he said softly, though his voice had a scraping edge to it.

Ann's tightly clogged lungs clamored for air. "You're out of line."

"I know."

She tore her gaze from him, stared out the window and fought for composure.

After a moment Drew said in a cooler tone, "So what did you buy?"

Relief made Ann weak. She sagged against the door. "I didn't shop for me."

"Then who did you shop for?"

"The baby."

"Baby? Whose baby?"

"Mine."

Nine

"*Yours!*" His jaw dropped like an anvil. "What the hell?"

Ann couldn't suppress a quick smile. When she'd blurted her news about the baby, she hadn't realized how it must have sounded. Women were openly bearing children out of wedlock these days, and while not totally accepted by society, it no longer had the stigma attached it once had.

But that wasn't what had brought about his flabbergasted reaction, she surmised. It was the thought that she had a child and hadn't bothered to tell him.

"Actually, they're for the baby I'm hoping to get," she said, breaking the heavy silence.

Drew continued to stare at her as if she had indeed gone off the deep end, his blue eyes dark and inquiring.

"Don't look at me like that," she said.

"Get? You said get." He didn't bother to conceal his impatience.

"If you'll just give me time, I'll explain." Ann's impatience now matched his.

"I'm listening."

"I want to adopt a child." She smiled again. "In fact, I've applied to a state agency."

"You can't be serious."

Ann's smile disappeared, and she stiffened. "Rest assured, I'm serious."

"Why, that's the craziest thing I've ever heard."

"I don't recall asking for your opinion."

"Surely you haven't thought this through."

Ann gritted her teeth. Her eyes flashed. "Of course I've thought it through. Adoption is the best for me."

"Well, in my opinion, that's taking a big risk." His tone was harsh. "Oh, I know they screen the babies, but in the end there always seem to be problems."

A chill passed through Ann. "I happen not to agree."

"If you want to have a baby, why the hell don't you just get married and have your own baby?"

Her face turned ashen, and she clasped her hands together. "Why don't *you* mind your own business?"

"I just don't get it," he said, removing a hand from the steering wheel and raking his fingertips through his hair.

"I don't care if you get it or not." Fury shook her voice.

Drew took his eyes off the road again and gave her another long, probing look. "You're really serious about this, aren't you?"

"Yes."

"Why?" His voice sounded strained.

"I want a baby, a child, that's why."

"Can't you have one of your own? I mean, is there something wrong?"

His question hit her with the subtlety of a baseball bat over the head and shattered her control. Blood rushed to her cheeks. "Go to hell."

He eyed her oddly, then smiled, a smile that spread into laughter. "I still think you're crazy, but if that's what makes you happy...."

Ann kept her eyes straight ahead. How dare he treat her like this, as though she were a nitwit? It was all she could do to keep from reaching out and smacking his smug face. "Don't you dare make fun of me."

"Look—"

"Forget it. I don't think we have anything else to say to each other."

Drew swore aloud, then faced the road and said no more.

Ann lifted her shoulders up and down, then crossed her right hand to her left shoulder and massaged it. She couldn't remember when she'd ever been so tired. Part of her fatigue stemmed from physical labor and part from mental stress.

The last customer had gone for the day, even though it was only four o'clock. Ann was alone; Sophie had walked to the café across the street to grab a bite to eat. Four boxes of supplies had arrived earlier, and Sophie had promised to help her check them in and stock them on the shelves.

"Ugh!" Ann muttered, when she caught a glimpse of the boxes stacked inside the beautician room.

She got up from behind her worktable, stretched, then continued to rub her shoulders. Boy, was she tired. The weather was terrible; rain had fallen all day. Maybe that was why business had been so good. Both she and Sophie had been busy.

She was thrilled, of course, but it had been an effort to be cheery and chat with the customers. She'd felt slightly brain-dead all day.

Oh, who was she trying to kid? She'd been in a state, not just today, but ever since Drew had made her feel like a fool for wanting to adopt a child.

Damn him.

It was three days after the fact, and she still hadn't forgiven him. She doubted she ever would. Things happened for the best, her mother had always told her. Well, she was certain this was for the best.

A home and family weren't in his vocabulary. And a child... Obviously that was a dirty word. In spite of the hard core of anger inside her, tears stung Ann's eyes. Why did he have to be so handsome? So charming? But such a cad.

She dashed the tears from her eyes, stiffened her spine and headed toward the boxes. If she ever wanted to get home and soak in the tub, she'd best stop feeling sorry for herself and get to work.

And face a few facts. Drew MacMillan had never been part of her life, and he never would be. She was going to have to come to terms with that.

Ann was halfway to the room when she heard the buzzer indicating that the shop's front door was open. Knowing it was too soon for Sophie to return, she stopped and swung around.

"Hello, sis."

"Peter?"

"One in the same."

Ann blinked twice to make sure her brother wasn't a ghost. But he was no ghost; he stood before her in the flesh. Months had passed since she'd seen him. He hadn't changed, except maybe his weight. He looked heavier, which wasn't a plus to his already sturdy frame. Other than that, his hazel-colored eyes still had that dull, mistrusting glint in them, and the lock of dark hair that continually fell across his forehead was there, as well. His perfect white teeth were his best feature, but they weren't in evidence as he wasn't smiling.

"What . . . what brings you back?"

"Now, is that anyway to greet your long-lost brother?"

"No, it isn't," she said flatly, feeling the threat of tears again. "I should be hugging you. But you've made that impossible, haven't you?"

He sneered. "Don't start that bull. I'm not in the mood."

"What do you want?" she asked coldly.

"Money."

"How stupid of me. Why else would you be here?" Ann vacillated between tears and anger.

Peter came toward her. "I'm in a jam."

"No!" she cried. "Don't come any closer."

Peter's mouth twisted. But before he could say anything, Ann added, "This well has dried up."

"Dammit, I need money to pay off a loan shark."

"Have you ever thought about getting a job?"

"A *job*." Peter spat the word as though it were a dreaded disease. "There's no time. I need the money now."

"Not from me you don't."

He took a step closer. "Now, see here—"

"I don't have the money, Peter. Even if I could give it to you, I wouldn't. What cash I had is in that room in there." She pointed toward the beautician room. "So you see, you'll have to go elsewhere for help."

Peter's features turned menacing. "I bet I know where you can get the money."

"Oh, and where is that?" she demanded sarcastically.

"Your boyfriend." His lips curled with contempt.

"My boyfriend?" she echoed blankly.

"Yeah, Drew MacMillan."

Her nerve endings rang in warning, rendering her speechless. Then she recovered and laughed. "Whoever gave you that information is dead wrong."

"I don't think so. He's loaded. Get it from him."

Ann gasped. "Didn't you hear what I said? Anyway, where did you get the idea he'd give *me* money?"

"Word has it around town that you're his latest 'bimbette.' And I believe it."

Ann swallowed around the tightness in her throat. "How . . . how long have you been here?"

"Long enough."

"Well," she said, ignoring the alarm that shook her voice. "You can forget it. And just to set the record straight, Drew MacMillan is the last person I would approach for money. Even if I were to ask, he wouldn't give it to me."

"Damn you, I'm in no mood to play games."

The uneasiness inside her dissipated. Only pity and a numbness remained. "I'm not, either. You disgust me. Just go. Just get out of my sight."

"Not until I get what I came for."

"Oh, for heaven's . . ."

Peter bolted toward her, his face a thundercloud.

Ann couldn't move; her limbs were paralyzed. Her heart pounded, and her lungs clamored for oxygen.

The buzzer sounded.

Frightened of her brother for the first time in her life, Ann went weak with relief.

"Ann, what on earth—" Sophie broke off. Her eyes darted from Ann to Peter.

"I'll be back," Peter said tersely. Then he whipped around and skirted past Sophie. He slammed the door behind him, and the room seemed to rock.

"Whew!" Sophie exclaimed, her eyes huge in her small face. "What was that all about?"

Ann bit down on her lower lip to stop it from trembling. "You don't want to know."

"Yes, I do."

Ann took a long breath before she said, "That was Peter."

"Your brother?"

"My brother."

"Good Lord. You all right?"

Ann nodded mutely.

"Want to tell me what this is all about?"

"Oh, Soph, it's a long, heartbreaking story. But the short of it is, since he couldn't play football, he's drifted in and out of trouble and from one job to another." She paused and stared into space. "And to think he was once such an adorable kid."

"Unfortunately, adorable kids sometimes grow up to be hellions. So, what does he want from you?"

"Money, which I refused to give him."

"This just hasn't been your week, has it? First Drew made you see red, now this."

Ann hadn't intended to tell Sophie about her day spent in Drew's company, but after he'd upset her so and after she'd moped around the shop for two days, Sophie had pulled the truth out of her.

"I guess you can't win them all," Ann finally said with false bravado.

"Ah, blow 'em both off. We both know that men are pains in the royal rear." Sophie shrugged. "Feed 'em fish heads and rice, my daddy used to say."

"Oh, Sophie, you're the best friend a person could have."

"Think so, huh?"

Ann laughed through her tears. "I know so."

"Then come here, you little idiot, and let me give you a hug."

Ten

——

"**W**ill that be all, Mr. MacMillan?"

Drew lifted the floral box filled with a dozen long-stemmed red roses and smiled at a retired ex-teacher of his who worked part-time at the florist. "That's all today, Ms. Epps. But I'm sure I'll be seeing you again, soon."

She chuckled. "You young boys are all alike, a new girl on the string every day."

Drew's lips twitched. "Well, I'm hardly a boy, Ms. Epps, but thanks for the compliment anyway."

A few minutes later, Drew sat in his Jag and eyed the box on the seat next to him.

Would she accept the roses? Would she see him? The latter was what he worried about and not the damn roses.

He owed her an apology, pure and simple. But that wasn't the only reason for the flowers. Wherever he turned, he saw Ann's face. And tasted her lips, just made for kissing. After sampling those, he'd known he couldn't stay away.

So why had he acted like a jerk and taken issue with her about adopting a baby? She wanted a kid? Hell, let her get one. It was no sweat off his back, nor was it any of his business.

He didn't want to marry her, but he sure as hell wanted her.

Following their disagreement, he'd tried to tell himself she didn't matter, that he'd get over the aching in his gut. He'd worked on his daddy's business, gone through the motions of doing what had been required of him, but it hadn't worked.

He wanted Ann so much it made him physically ill, sick to his stomach. That loss of control angered him. He couldn't remember when something had gotten to him this badly, when he'd been so emotional or so undisciplined. But then he believed she was only a passing fancy, that this obsession would either temper or fade altogether. It hadn't. At first, she presented a challenge to see what smoldered beneath her calm facade, and he took pride in never backing down from a challenge. Even so, he capitulated with the ease of a child being offered a new toy.

Maybe if he slept with her, he'd lick his fixation once and for all.

He nosed the Jag in the direction of Ann's house, his burden much lighter.

* * *

Ann's head pounded. It felt as if two snare drums were battling inside. As she let herself into the house, one thing was on her mind: relief.

She tossed her purse on the couch, then dropped her tote bag on the floor. It was then she realized she wasn't alone. She spun around. Her heart dropped to her toes.

"What are you doing here? What do you want?" she demanded in what she hoped was a strong voice.

Her brother sat on the couch in the shadows, nonchalantly, his legs sprawled in front of him. He appeared not to have a care in the world. Ann knew better. She saw that look in his eyes—the same look he'd had as a little boy when he hadn't gotten his way.

Well, he was sadly mistaken if he thought she was going to placate him. He hadn't been able to bully her in those days, and he wasn't going to now. He should have realized that at the shop. Still, she felt another tiny ripple of fear. Stop acting silly, she scolded herself. He's your brother, for god's sake. When it comes down to it, he's not going to hurt you.

"I see you finally got home," Peter said, watching as Ann ventured deeper into the room.

"I asked you what you wanted." Her tone was cold and flat.

"Same thing I wanted when I came to the shop."

Ann lifted her chin. "And the same thing still applies. I don't have the money, and even if I did, I wouldn't give it to you."

Peter stood, then yawned.

"My God, Peter, look at you. Unshaven. Dirty. How can you do this to yourself? You need help."

"I didn't come here for a sermon," he hissed, closing the distance between them. "I told you to ask Drew. By god, he owes me!"

"You poor misguided fool." Pity shown from Ann's eyes. "Join the real world. People like Drew don't owe anyone. They owe *him*."

"If I don't get the money, I'm going to be in real trouble."

"Oh, Peter," Ann said dully, "how many times have I heard that?"

"It's different this time," he said in a faint, slightly cajoling tone.

Ann squared her shoulders and prayed for strength. He'd duped her so many times, hurt her so deeply, that she had to remain strong. If she kept bailing him out of trouble, he'd never learn. But the thought of anyone hurting him, physically, didn't bear thinking about.

"Sis..."

"Get a job, Peter. That's the only answer. Tell them you'll pay them back a little at a time."

"Dammit, there isn't time for all that. I have to have the money within a week."

"The answer is still no," she whispered, blinking back the threat of tears.

"Where's your purse?" Peter's angry eyes swept the room. When he spotted her purse on the couch, he rushed toward it.

"What are you doing!" Ann cried, and dashed after him.

By the time she reached him, he had her purse open and was rummaging through it.

"Stop it!" She jerked on his arm. "I told you I don't have the kind of money you need."

Peter's eyes glittered dangerously. "Where's your checkbook?"

"No!"

"Yes!" He dropped the purse, reached for her and shook her.

"Peter . . . no!" she cried again.

"What the hell!"

They both froze at the sound of Drew's voice. She and Peter had been so involved in their argument that they hadn't heard the door open. "Take your hands off of her," Drew said.

His tone of voice gave his words a more ominous ring than if he'd shouted them.

Peter's arms tightened around Ann. "Go to hell!"

Drew tossed aside the flowers and lunged for Peter. Peter let go of Ann; she stumbled backward. Drew shoved Peter against the wall.

"Don't, Drew!"

Drew stopped in midaction. He dropped Peter—as if he were a sack of garbage. But Drew didn't back away. He remained in front of Peter's face and said with icy softness, "If you ever lay a hand on your sister again, you'll be sorry."

"You don't scare me," Peter replied, his tone sneering.

But Ann knew he was scared. A pulse thumped in his Adam's apple, and sweat covered his face. One on one, Peter was no match for Drew.

"What are you doing here, anyway?" Drew demanded. "Hope it's not to ask for money."

"It is," Ann put in. "He's after money for his gambling debt. I already told him I didn't have it, but he wouldn't take no for an answer."

"Well, you'll damn well take no for an answer now and get out of here."

Peter's expression darkened. "You can't order me around. It's for Ann to say whether I go or not."

"I suggest you rethink that last statement," Drew said, his tone once again even, but with that ominous ring to it.

"Stop it, both of you! Stop it right this minute." Tears blinded Ann, and she wiped them away with an angry gesture.

Peter looked at both of them for a moment, then stomped to the door, walked out and slammed it behind him.

Ann couldn't speak, nor could she move. Her bones felt too brittle. She could only stand there while the tears washed her face.

"Don't," Drew groaned, then strode toward her, stopping close enough that their breaths mingled.

But he didn't touch her. He looked at her, and she saw raw, naked desire in his eyes. She trembled violently, and he drew her into his arms.

"Shh, don't cry," he said, holding her against him for the longest time. Only after she sighed and nestled closer did his lips slowly but hungrily trail across her cheek, drinking the tears, possessing her mouth.

Like a frightened doe on the run, Ann's heart beat inside. His tongue meshed with hers in its quest to inflame and conquer.

"Drew," she murmured weakly, half in protest, half in submission, but he wasn't listening. His attention was focused on tugging her blouse free of her jeans and getting to the flesh underneath. She heard his sharp intake of breath when he unclasped her bra and his hand came in contact with her breast. His hand couldn't contain its fullness as she swelled under his touch.

Moisture flooded Ann's body, and she sagged against him, the tug-of-war on her nipple almost more than she could stand.

He pressed the length of him against her, and she felt his hardness. "God...I want you...." he choked out. "Now."

I want you, too, she cried silently, only not like this, not in the heat of the moment. "No...I can't." Ann broke out of his arms. "No...I can't," she gasped. "No...please...not like this."

She needed his comfort, needed to feel his arms around her. The time had been so right for that. But for anything else, the time had been so wrong. Lust was not the answer. That wasn't what she wanted from Drew. Not a quick, meaningless roll in the hay. And for Drew, that would be all it would mean.

He let her go. The arms that dropped to his side were as tight as steel bands; the muscles shuddered as if he was suffering withdrawal pains.

"Dammit, Ann, I..." He couldn't go on.

Their eyes locked. Questions hung in the air, thick and heavy. Questions neither dared voice.

"You...you don't have to say anything," she whispered. "I...understand. Please just go."

"You sure you'll be all right?" Drew asked at last, though his voice sounded rusty and his breathing wasn't quite right.

"I'll...be fine."

His eyes continued to probe hers for a long moment.

She shifted her gaze to the pathetic bouquet that she only vaguely remembered him tossing aside.

"Thanks...for the flowers," she said just as she reached the door, hating for him to leave her but knowing there was no other way.

He swung around; his lips hinted at a smile. "The flowers look kind of sad, don't they?"

"Water will take care of that."

They fell silent, but sparks still flew between them. Her skin felt scorched from them.

"Why...did you bring them?" Ann asked in a barely audible tone, her eyes finding his once again. "The flowers, I mean."

He gave her his heart-tugging, lopsided grin. "My way of apologizing for acting like an ass the other day."

Ann looked startled. Drew apologizing? She couldn't believe it. "I think we both got out of line. We'll just leave it at that, okay?"

"You're sure you'll be all right?" he repeated.

She could feel his body lure her, pull at her. She hugged cold hands to her side. "I'm...sure."

Only she hadn't been sure. She hadn't been sure about anything, she told herself later, in bed, as she stared at the ceiling. She wouldn't ever be sure of anything, not as long as Drew remained in Mac-Millan.

Another sliver of pain darted through her head. But she simply didn't have the energy to get up and take anything. So she lay still and gave in to the flood of emotions that assailed her. Confusion? Desire? Need? Which one described what she felt toward Drew?

The emotion she had taken pains to bypass inadvertently jumped to the forefront of her mind. Love? The thought stabbed her like a sharp knife. No, absolutely not. He was just a forbidden temptation, a forbidden fling. When she fell in love, it would be with someone whose goals and life-style matched hers.

Anyway, she had better sense than to do anything that stupid.

Eleven

Ann knew she was a glutton for punishment. Continuing to see Drew proved that. But she was smitten. No, she was addicted to his volatile personality and lopsided smile. She couldn't reconcile her out-of-character behavior, so she refused to dwell on it.

She simply savoured the time spent with him. Since the night of the brouhaha with Peter, she had gone to dinner with Drew, then to a movie in nearby Lufkin. Though he hadn't touched her—he'd gone out of his way to avoid doing so—the electricity had been there, exposed, ready to burst into flames without warning.

The intimacy had alarmed her, and excited her. Waking each morning had never held such pleasure. Her liaison with Drew hadn't been all that contributed to her happiness; she'd gone to Austin for the orientation session at the agency.

She hadn't told Drew; it hadn't been necessary. He'd spent the same two days in Houston. Besides, she hadn't wanted anything to mar her trip. The experience had been one she'd never forget.

The meeting had begun with Ann and several couples being introduced to the agency staff, followed by a panel of prospective birth mothers. But what had impressed her the most, had been the tour of the facility with emphasis on the maternity wing.

"Take a good look," Dorothy Sable had said with a smile. "Because this is the last time you'll be allowed in this section."

"Why?" Ann asked shyly.

"By then there might be a chance that you'd come in contact with the birth mother of your child."

When Dorothy said "your child," panicked excitement shot through Ann.

Afterward, they had returned to the meeting room for a question-and-answer session. In all, it had been a wonderful day, and she was reassured that she was doing the right thing.

The only shadow in her life was Peter. Despite her efforts not to, she constantly worried about him. He was her brother, after all, her only surviving kin, and the thought of some creep breaking his leg or worse, caused her deep pain and remorse. Had she done right in refusing to bail him out of trouble again? Drew had assured her that she had. Still . . .

Now, as Ann pilfered through her tote bag for her ledger, thoughts of Peter kept intervening. She had

closed the shop early because of the funeral for another of the town's leading citizens. Her two customers scheduled for late afternoon had canceled.

Tonight she was to have dinner at Drew's house,
and her exhilaration was building. But first things
first, she told herself, taking everything out of the bag,
certain she'd brought home the ledger.

When she didn't find it, she pursed her lips and
thought for a moment. Her mind's eye saw it at the
shop, on the desk in the pedicure room.

"Drat," she muttered, knowing she'd have to dash
back to the shop and get it. She had to post today or
get further behind. Without any more fuss, she made
the short trip downtown.

When she first opened the door, she didn't notice
anything amiss or even different. What she did notice, however, was an eerie quiet.

She paused on the threshold, switched on the light
to counteract the cloud cover outside, then gasped.
"Oh, no!"

The shop's interior looked like war-torn Beirut.
Judging from where she stood, the room appeared as
if nothing had escaped the intruder's vengeance. Tears
blinded her as she stood helplessly silent. Who could
have done this? Who could have wrought such stark
destruction? And for what?

Unwittingly, thoughts of Peter rose to her mind.
Oh, God, no, please don't let him be responsible. If
that were the case, she didn't know how she would
survive the blow.

Finally, Ann decided that wallowing in self-pity was
not the answer, and she forced herself to cross the

room to the phone. Blinking back tears, she dialed the police, then Drew. She groped for the chair, sat down and swallowed the huge lump in her throat. The tears she'd tried to hold back soaked her face.

"Oh, Drew, you can't mean it?"

Drew stood by powerless and watched his mother's self-control crumble. "I don't have the proof yet," Drew said, easing down beside her on the couch. "But I expect to have it soon."

"But... Tim Pollard... why, he's been a family friend forever."

"I know, Mamma," Drew said. He took her cold hand in his and squeezed it.

He hadn't planned to say anything to her about the mess until he had proof one way or the other. But Janet had been feeling much better lately and had gone to the beauty shop. She'd heard the gossip.

His mother had confronted him with what she'd heard, and he'd had no choice but to be honest with her.

"I'll just pray that it won't be true," she said in an unsteady voice.

"Me, too, Mamma, me too."

"So is Ann coming to dinner?" Janet asked, changing the subject and sounding much stronger.

Drew got up, peered down at her and smiled. "Yep."

"Good. I always liked her. Thought she was made of the right stuff, especially in light of what she's been through."

The maid appeared just inside the door of the den before Drew could answer. "Mr. MacMillan, there's a phone call for you. The lady says it's urgent."

"Thanks, Maggie," Drew said with a frown, and strode to the phone nearby. "MacMillan here." He listened, and the color slowly left his face. "I'll be right there."

"What was that all about?" Janet asked.

"I'm afraid Ann won't be coming to dinner, after all," he said tersely. "Her shop's been broken into."

"Well, for heaven's sake," Janet said, and placed her hand to her chest. "Who would do a thing like that in MacMillan?"

"Don't know." Drew's tone was frigid. "But I aim to find out or see that the police do." He bent down and kissed his mother on the cheek. "I'll call you later."

Drew arrived at the shop at the same time the police did. Ann stood by the door, tracks of dried tears on her face. He longed to pull her into his arms, but of course he couldn't. He had to settle for taking a cold limp hand in his and warming it.

"Oh, Drew," she whispered, her bottom lip quivering. "I can't believe this."

"Shh, take it easy."

"Ma'am, I'm Officer Riley. I need to ask you some questions."

Drew removed his hand from Ann's and introduced himself to the young, green-eyed rookie.

Recognition lit his eyes. "Gee, Mr. MacMillan, I'm pleased to meet you. I keep up with you on the racetrack. I think you're a real fine driver."

"Thanks, I appreciate that," Drew said, with enough impatience that the officer realized he was off base.

"Sorry," he said, red-faced. "Now, Ms. Sinclair, is there anything missing?"

"No, not that I can tell."

"Do you know anyone who would do this?"

Drew sensed her hesitation, but only for a moment.

"My...my brother and I had a disagreement." She took a deep breath.

Drew knew what it must have cost her to implicate Peter. And like her, he didn't want to believe that his childhood friend could do anything so vindictive, so desperate. Yet he had to keep in mind that Peter had tried to manhandle Ann. If he'd do that, he'd do anything. And if he turned out to be the perpetrator here, Drew would like nothing better than to thrash him within an inch of his life for putting Ann through hell.

Drew stopped his thoughts from wandering and paid attention while Officer Riley asked Ann several more questions. Another officer dusted for fingerprints. At last he and Ann were left alone. Ann folded her arms across her chest as if to protect herself from the evil that had penetrated the premise.

"I feel so violated," she said, and stared at him, her lashes glazed with fresh tears.

"Anyone would in this situation," he responded.

Drew guessed she was about to break. She was holding herself together by a mere thread. Again, he steeled himself not to haul her into his arms and promise her that everything was going to be all right.

"And I feel so awful about implicating Peter, like I'm betraying him."

"Hey, stop beating up on yourself. You had to tell the truth."

"But what if he didn't do this?"

"Well, if he didn't, and that's a big if, mind you, then he'll be exonerated."

"I wish it were that simple." She let out a deep sigh. "He'd never forgive me."

"There's nothing to forgive," Drew said, deciding he'd best take her home before she retracted everything she'd told the police.

"I'm—"

"Come on," Drew interrupted brusquely, "let's get out of here."

Ann gripped her hands together. "I can't just leave this mess."

"Yes, you can. I'll take care of it. The insurance company needs to be notified. And I'll call a buddy of mine right now who owns a janitorial service out of Lufkin. My guess is that he'll have a crew here first thing in the morning. He owes me a favor."

Ann's eyes were huge in her pale face. "All...right, but tell him to contact me. I'll need to help supervise." She paused, surveyed the damage, then folded her arms over her chest as if to ward off a sudden chill.

"Dear God," she whispered, "what a mess. What a miserable, infuriating mess."

"Whoa, don't crash on me now," Drew said again, still refusing to touch her. "You've been doing great. As soon as I make that call, we'll go. We'll get your car tomorrow."

Ann didn't say anything, nor did she talk on the way home. Only after she entered the softly lamp-lighted room did she turn to him and say, "Thanks...for coming to my rescue. I'm fine now."

She was still visibly shaken, her tone unconvincing. Drew stifled a groan. "You're welcome—that goes without saying. But you're not fine."

An awkward silence followed.

He broke it. "Mother's sorry you couldn't come to dinner, and about the break-in, of course," Drew said, scrambling to counteract the heat building in the room. Or was the heat inside *him?*

"Tell her I'll take a rain check on dinner," Ann responded, a slight tremor in her voice.

"Look, I'd better go and let you get some rest." The lines around Drew's mouth deepened, and he spoke in a bleak, throbbing whisper.

Something flashed in Ann's eyes. Was it panic? He didn't know.

"Sleep. I wish that were possible."

He remained silent and stared at her, at her throat where her pulse beat as steadily as a tiny drum. "I'll call you later."

"Don't go, please."

He shoved his hands through his hair. "Do you know what you're saying?" he asked in a harsh, ragged voice.

"Yes." She reached out then and splayed a hand across his chest.

Her touch, even through his clothing, sent sparks blazing through him. His loins tightened.

Her gaze was wide and questioning. "Drew..."

What willpower he had left completely deserted him. He yanked her against him and ignored the warning bell that clanged inside his head. Don't think, Drew. Make the most of the moment.

He'd already partaken from the forbidden fruit and he'd just as soon die than stop now. He was tired of the ache in his gut from wanting to touch her like this, to explore the delights her lips had hinted at the other night. He had never experienced the raw desire that he felt for her.

How could he have backed himself into such a corner? How could he need her above all else? Before, he'd needed no one but himself.

"I tried not to want you," he whispered, his eyes filled with longing. "But by god, I do. I want to touch you. I want you to touch me."

His lips covered hers, and Ann collapsed against him, having lost the will to walk away. They were trapped in a fire of their own making. Everything else was of no importance. Recriminations would surely follow. But for now, the rich taste of him was all there was.

Her mouth parted and received his tongue; she felt it war with hers. Her back arched, and her breasts crushed against him. He was her lifeline; she must have his strength, his power. Yet her legs felt weighted down, as if she were standing in concrete. A throb developed between her thighs, and she had trouble breathing.

Drew opened her blouse. His hands surrounded a breast and kneaded it. An animal cry tore from her, and she moaned as his lips trapped a nipple and sucked. She wanted to know his body, to bring him the same pleasure.

When she tugged at his shirt, he pulled back and muttered, "I'll do it. It'll be faster."

Clothes were discarded, and once they were naked, Drew grabbed her with a fierceness that both thrilled and terrified her. But after they sank to the carpet and her fingers boldly circled his hot hardness, the terror fled. Only heady anticipation remained.

"Ann, oh, Ann," he groaned, as he entered her moist flesh with throbbing urgency.

They cried out simultaneously, and Drew stroked deeper. Pinpoints of ecstasy swept through them as their liquid union plunged them into a vortex that neither wanted to end. Their feverishness was edged with a painful holding back.

Ann was filled; her hands clutched at his back and buttocks. "Oh, yes, yes!"

His mouth sank into the hollow at her throat, the sides of her neck, her ears before halting on a breast where he again assaulted its fullness with his tongue.

Ann almost fainted with pleasure. Her eyelashes fluttered, and she whimpered as she gave into the friction that centered in her lower belly. Her hips convulsed inward again and again, and she felt the answering tautness in him. She gripped him until her fingers turned white.

Then he made a guttural sound and spasmed while they both hovered on the brink of ecstasy before tumbling headlong into that endless moment.

Twelve

—

Exhausted but sated, Ann rested her head against Drew. His heart hummed in her ear; its cadence beat the same pace as hers. It was as if this oneness she now felt with him gave her insight as to how his mind worked; his likes and dislikes, what angered him, made him happy, made him sad, and frightened him. To indulge herself like this was absurd, she knew, but for the moment, she couldn't stop.

She wanted to know everything about this man who made her body hum as none other ever had or ever would. But she was a realist. This moment in his arms was merely plucked out of time, never to be repeated. She prayed she was wrong.

"Are you awake?" he asked.

"Barely." She spread her hand across his stomach. The hairs there tickled her palm. He placed his hand over hers. Their coming together so suddenly, so urgently, had erased the awkwardness, the shyness.

"Ann."

"Mmm." Even his deep, coarse voice had the power to stir her.

"Did I ever tell you how sorry I was . . . am about your daddy?"

Ann went still, and her heart constricted. She hadn't expected this. "No, no you didn't."

"Well, I am."

"Thanks," she whispered, the one word scraping past the raw spot in her throat. She tried not to think about her daddy, for doing so always brought on tears and regrets.

"I tried to tell my daddy that he was making a big mistake." Ann felt his muscles tense under her hand. "But as you and everybody else know, you couldn't tell John MacMillan a damn thing. He thought he knew it all."

Drew paused, shifted his position slightly so that he could look into her face. "You know, the worst part about it is he went to his grave feeling the same way."

"No," Ann whispered. "The worst part is that the two of you never reconciled."

"I tried, but he never budged." His voice was a monotone, expressionless. "Everything had to be his way or not at all."

"That's too bad."

"If it hadn't been for my mother . . ."

He didn't have to say anything more. Ann understood. "Mine, too. She was my rock until she got sick. If medical science is right about stress causing cancer, then Mother was a clear-cut case. Peter's escapades kept her tied in knots."

Drew's eyes were bleak. "I'm sorry as hell about that, too. I'd give anything if that accident hadn't happened."

"The accident wasn't your fault. And I don't blame you for my daddy or Peter. Life just decides to kick us in the teeth sometimes, and we never know why."

"Deep down you think Peter trashed your shop, don't you?"

"Yes, and it tears me up to think that he is so desperate." Her eyes glazed over. "Maybe if I'd given in and helped him one more time."

"Don't...don't say it—don't even think it. He's got to learn that he can't run to you every time he gets in a jam."

"You're right. But when I think of my beautiful shop..." Her voice broke.

His hold tightened. "Hey, your shop's going to be in good shape, you'll see. You'll have to replace some supplies and that glass stuff for sure. But at least it'll be straight and clean. You can bet on it."

"Poor, poor Peter."

"Yeah, maybe if I'd been the one hurt that day this would have never happened. I never planned to play pro ball."

"What is this, true confession time?" Ann teased, hoping to remove that bleakness from his eyes and to lighten the dark mood that had settled over them. Yet she'd glimpsed a side of Drew she'd never seen before. His sincerity and vulnerability touched her.

As if sensing he'd shown too much of his inner self, he switched on his I-don't-give-a-damn-charm and grinned. "You're right, enough of this confession malarkey. We've got more important things pressing."

"Such as?"

His eyes darkened as he circled a breast with the tip of one finger. "Beautiful. So beautiful."

"They're too big," she said with a boldness that shocked her.

"Never."

"Is that supposed to be a compliment?" she asked huskily.

"They're perfect." He put his lips to her nipple.

She squirmed.

"Feel that?"

"Yes, down to my toes. Oh...."

He chuckled before moving his mouth to her face, to the corners of her eyes that were sensitive and smooth as silk. He kissed her there, then, with a heartfelt sigh sank his head between her breasts and licked the rising tops of her breasts.

"Oh, Drew," she whispered, arching toward him, wanting him again.

"Don't you think we ought to find a bed?"

They hadn't moved since they'd drifted to the thick carpet.

"Do you?" she asked, finding it hard to concentrate as his mouth continued to do strange things to her body.

"No," he said thickly. "I'm not sure I could walk, anyway."

"Me, either. But aren't you uncomfortable? I mean . . ."

He chuckled again. "You needn't worry about my knees because this time, you're going to be on top."

With that, he pulled her over him. Ann sucked in her breath, and her eyes widened when he lifted her and slid high into her. Her thighs parted, then closed around him.

He muttered incoherently, positioning his hands at her waist while they both moved.

Ah, perfect. The sensation of what they were sharing jarred something loose inside her, like running nude on the beach on a moonlit night. Ann's heart soared as she hurled tempestuously toward the ultimate ending, the sweet meshing of flesh and emotion into one.

He cried out suddenly and heaved, and she felt him shudder as he thrust higher into her. She heard her own cry the instant everything inside her shattered, as if she'd just walked blindly into a mirror.

"Oh, Drew," she sobbed, and fell against his chest.

Later, they did make it to her bed and actually slept. Now sunlight eked through the blinds and awakened Ann. At first she felt disoriented as she stretched and experienced an unfamiliar soreness. Then she remembered. Her eyes popped open, and she sat straight up in bed.

Drew walked back into the bedroom, his discarded clothes clutched in one hand. Her mouth went instantly dry. He was still naked. And though she had touched every part of that rock-hard body, the sight of him in full view sent her pulses skyrocketing again.

"Good morning," he said without modesty, as if he made a habit of parading around naked.

"Hi," she murmured.

"I'd about decided you were going to sleep all morning," he said, a glint in his eyes.

"Er... what time is it?"

He glanced at his Rolex. "Eight."

"Eight!" she exclaimed. "I have a set of 'falsies' to put on at nine."

"Come again?"

Ann's cheeks turned scarlet. "Oh."

Drew laughed outright. "I can't believe you're embarrassed."

"Actually, what I meant to say was that I have a set of false nails to put on a lady."

Her prim tone garnered a deep-throated chuckle from Drew.

She returned his smile, only to then feel it fade, thoughts of the break-in intruding. "Do you think I'll be able to work?"

"You may have to run to the store and buy some supplies, but other than that, I don't see why not."

Her face cleared somewhat. "The storage closet wasn't touched. I'm positive I have some polish in there."

They were quiet for a moment.

"'Falsies,' huh?" Drew said at last, and scratched his head. "That's a good one. Yeah, I'll have to remember that."

"Oh, you!" She threw a pillow at him. It hit him square in the face, then ricocheted to the floor.

He looked at her, stunned. "Bulls-eye."

They both laughed. Then the laughter died as a more potent, more powerful emotion took its place. An intimacy that surpassed words blazed between them, merged them as one, again.

"Ann..."

"Yes?" she whispered achingly. Her body stiffened against the tumultuous emotions he always created in her.

Drew looked away, and the spell broke. But he was affected, too. A pulse hammered in his jaw; the hand he slipped through the arm of his shirt shook.

Yet Ann couldn't bring herself to ask the question that hovered over her like a dark cloud threatening to blemish the moment. Would she see him again? Or was this the typical one-night stand that he was so famous for?

Don't whine, Ann, she ordered herself brutally. After all, she reminded herself, she had known the score when she'd chosen this path. She knew she was flirting with heartbreak. Even if they both wanted a relationship, it wouldn't work. She was settled; he was unsettled. He was wealthy; she was just the opposite. He lived on the edge; she walked the straight and narrow. He broke the rules; she followed them.

He pulled on his jeans and buckled his belt. Her gaze focused on his hands, hands that had explored the roads of her body, slowly, thoroughly, with a delicious wantonness.

It hit her then. She had done the worst thing imaginable. She had fallen in love. Or possibly, she had loved him all along. Her stomach lurched, and the only reason she didn't cry out was that she bit her lower lip.

"I'll be by the shop later, okay?"

He stared at her, his eyes smoldering with passion.

"Okay." The word came out a mere whisper.

He turned his back on her and walked toward the front door.

"I love you." There, she'd said it, spilled the words like a glass of forbidden wine.

Only he hadn't heard her. The room beyond was empty.

Thirteen

"What are you doing here?"

The words shattered the long-standing silence.

She whirled and faced him with startled eyes. "Jeez, you scared me," she said. She placed her hand over her heart as if to quiet it.

"Didn't mean to." Drew moseyed toward her. "I thought the shop was closed on Mondays."

"It is, but Kay, my new hairstylist, is fixing a lady's hair." Ann pointed to the back. "They're in there."

"That doesn't explain what *you're* doing here."

Ann shrugged. "I'm straightening, something I've been doing since the break-in."

Three days had passed since that eventful day and night. She had been hard at work ever since. Though the janitorial service had done an exemplary job, only

Ann knew exactly where her supplies belonged. Thank goodness, the insurance had been quick to pay, enabling her to replace the glass displays and other items that had been broken.

Drew had even helped her, or tried to, on one occasion. But he'd ended up being more of a hindrance than a help, especially when he'd kept nuzzling her neck every chance he got. Finally, she'd chased him out, telling him she'd never get anything done with him around. But he'd seen the glazed look in her eyes and had sensed the rapid beat of her heart and knew she wanted him as much as he wanted her.

Now as he stood over her, he asked, "You planning to work all day?"

She paused and looked at him. "Probably."

"I don't think that's a good idea."

She raised her eyebrows. "Oh?"

He shrugged. "For starters, the weather's great and I don't want to work."

She gave him the once-over. "I can see that."

He had on a blue T-shirt, cutoffs and deck shoes. He grinned, then shrugged again. "I told you I'm not going to work."

Ann didn't respond, and his eyes tracked her as she took bottles of nail polish out of a box and placed them on a glass shelf.

He had to admire the way Ann met crises head-on. She didn't try to ignore or run from them. Maybe that was because she was organized and wanted everything perfect, a trait that became more evident as he watched her perform her task, her features pinched in concentration. Her hand moved with sure even strokes, in the same manner she'd stroked his body....

"So," he said quickly, into the mounting silence.

Ann peered at him from under a screen of lashes while a smile toyed with her lips. "So you don't want me to, either, huh?"

"Ah, finally the lady catches on."

Ann threw him an exasperated look before making her way to the pedicure room.

"Hey, where're you going?"

When she didn't answer, Drew followed her, mesmerized by the way the outfit she had on emphasized her derriere. The long fuchsia top failed to cover the enticing curve of her rounded buttocks.

He went hot all over.

"So what did you have in mind?" she asked just inside the room.

"This," Drew muttered, and grabbed her and pushed her against the wall.

"Drew!" she gasped, startled.

"Shh," he whispered, nudging her lips apart. "I've been wanting to do this ever since I walked in the door."

"Stop it," she pleaded, and wiggled against him. "Kay might see us."

"So what?"

He bent his head.

"Drew..." His name drowned in the hot moistness of his lips.

Ann sagged weakly against him and whimpered, even as she kissed him back. Only after his hand cupped a pulsating breast did she push him away and step out of harm's reach.

Drew sucked air deep into his lungs but still couldn't speak. He sneaked a look at her and finally managed to say, "What are those called you have on?"

She glanced down. "My...pants?"

"Yeah."

"Leggings."

His gaze skimmed over her again, devouring, possessive. "Nice."

"Er...thanks."

He heard the breathless quality of her voice and knew that he affected her the same way she affected him.

"Let's get out of here," he said, stifling a groan.

"And go where?"

"Oh, say a ride in my Jag." His eyes crinkled at the corners. "Ah, come on, be a sport."

Ann hesitated. "Oh, all right. Let me tell Kay."

A few minutes later, Ann sat buckled beside him. He didn't start the car. Instead he stared at her for a long moment. "There's something I want...have to ask you about the other night," he began, his voice sounding cottony, unused. He coughed and cursed himself as she visibly tensed.

But he had to say what had plagued him for days. He wanted to get it off his chest so as not to ruin the day. "I hope there're not going to be any repercussions...."

"Don't you mean you hope I'm not pregnant," she said bluntly, her face losing its color.

He exhaled deeply. "Yes, that's what I mean. But I blame myself. I should've taken precautions, only..." He let his sentence trail off, thinking that he'd been in too damn big of a hurry to bury himself inside her.

"You don't have to worry," she said, staring straight ahead. "It was the wrong time of the month."

He frowned. "I didn't think there ever was a wrong time of the month."

"I just finished my period." She faced him with wide unsettled eyes. "So you see, you're safe."

"And so are you, right?"

"Right," she said with a slight catch in her voice.

Drew gripped the steering wheel. Dammit, he knew she wanted a baby. But not his, for god's sake. Panic surged through him.

"I thought we were going for a drive."

Her flat voice prodded him out of his thoughts. He twisted the key and listened as the Jag's engine purred instantly. Still, he couldn't let the subject go. There was something niggling at the back of his mind. "I know you want a baby, Ann, but..."

She jerked her head around. "I know what you're thinking," she said rigidly, "but don't. I want a baby, but not yours."

He cursed at his fumbling again. "Sorry, I was out of line."

"Yes, you were."

Following a long silence, he reached over and stroked her cheek. "It's all right if you wanna knock me up side the head."

A smile flirted with her lips.

"Forgiven?" he asked, that devilish glint back in his eyes.

She faced him and smiled for real. "Yes, you big idiot."

He chuckled and gunned the engine. "You're gonna love this."

"I guess you're planning to show off."

"Like you've never seen before."

She rolled her eyes. "Did anyone ever tell you you're a cocky 'you know what'?"

A deep rumble came from his gut. "At least once a day."

"You're bad."

"I know." His warm gaze slid over her and rested on her breasts. His gut knotted at the same time her breathing turned shallow, as if she could read his mind.

"Don't . . . you think we ought to go?" Ann's face was flushed.

"Yeah, right."

Drew punched a button and the car's roof glided back. The sunlight poured through and danced across their skin.

"You couldn't have asked for a more perfect day for an outing."

"It is nice." Ann took a breath of fresh air. "And I needed the break."

Drew steered the car onto the highway. "You got that right."

"Where are we going?"

"Where do you want to go?"

Ann lifted her dainty shoulders. "This is your party, remember."

"We'll just drive for a while." He winked at her. "I'll show you how a Jag can perform."

They traveled in silence for a while, each lost in their own thoughts.

Finally, Ann asked, "Have you proved your case against Tim Pollard yet?"

"No. I'm still waiting to hear the final word from my buddy in Houston."

"I hope he can help."

"Me, too," Drew replied grimly. "I know the SOB's guilty, only I can't prove it. The company's just got to be more solvent than it shows."

"Have you told your mother?"

"Yes, and it shocked her."

"I can imagine."

"Meanwhile, dealership business is on hold." He didn't bother to curb his frustration. "I'm ready to get the hell back to Houston and stay."

"I'm sure," she said softly.

Only I don't want to leave you, he thought. Of course he couldn't say that aloud even as he felt her beside him like an extra beat of his heart. He cursed himself for being a fool.

What was happening to him, inside where he was so vulnerable? Strong, capable and loving was Ann Sinclair. She cared about him; he knew that. He had taken advantage of that, too. Ignoring the consequences, he had indulged his own needs. He wished it were that simple; it wasn't. The feelings she evoked in him were something new. And because he was waging war with himself, he was at a loss as to what to do.

"Mmm, this was a great idea," Ann mused, shattering the silence.

He faced her just as she tossed her head and laughed. He clamped down on the urge to touch her, experiencing that all-too-familiar kick in his gut. "Told you."

She grinned saucily. "You would."

Drew laughed.

They were now on a deserted road that seemed to stretch forever. He smashed the accelerator. The car shot forward.

"Drew!" Ann shrieked, her white knuckles curling around the edge of the seat.

"Drew, what?" he mimicked, excitement leaping from his eyes.

Ann's hair billowed around her face like a black silk cloud. She scraped a dozen strands off a cheek and out of her mouth before she could speak. "How...fast are you going?"

"Not fast enough, that's for sure."

Her excitement matched his. "You come alive behind a wheel, don't you?"

"It's almost as good as sex."

Ann snapped upright. "That's disgusting."

The wind tossed his laughter at her. "But truthful."

She gazed heavenward. "What you are is hopeless."

"Want me to show you what this lady can do?" He patted the steering wheel.

Ann hesitated. "All . . . right."

Drew shoved the Jag into another gear, then bore down on the pedal even more. The wildflowers and cattle grazing on the side, even the tall pines, blurred in the wake of the car's lightning speed.

But Drew scarcely noticed. He was on a high that nothing could touch, except sex. He smiled inwardly and stole a glance at Ann. He'd meant it when he'd told her racing brought the same feeling. Her response had been so prim, but he'd seen the smile hovering over her lips.

"Drew, don't you think you should slow down?"

He flashed her another quick look. "Hey, we're barely getting started."

She smiled, but it didn't stick. "Surely not. Surely this car can't go much faster." She sounded out of breath.

"Oh, but it can. I'll show you."

"No, I don't think that's a good idea."

"Ah, come on, where's your sense of adventure?" he demanded, watching as the speedometer climbed.

"Drew . . . please . . . stop," she begged in a whisper.

"Relax, baby, and enjoy the ride."

"I can't."

"Yes, you can. Trust me, okay?"

She seemed to take him at his word, and for a while they sped along the highway with the wind roaring in their ears.

"I was right, wasn't I?" he said, keeping his eyes straight ahead.

Silence.

Drew whipped his head in Ann's direction. Her face was a greenish gray, and her backbone was as rigid as an iron bar. "My God, are you all right?"

"Stop...stop the car," she choked out, "or I'm going to be sick."

A few seconds later, Drew wheeled the car into the shoulder of the road. His brow was knitted in concern.

"Are you all right?" he asked again.

"N-no...no," Ann stammered.

The abject fear in her eyes cut him to the bone. "You weren't kidding. You were scared." He opened his mouth to apologize only—

"Don't you ever pull a stunt like that again!"

The cold fury in her voice stunned him. "Hey, don't you think you're overreacting?"

"Overreacting!" she shrieked. "You're crazy!"

He tried to hold down the anger building inside him. "I know what I'm doing," he said patiently. "I'm a professional at this."

"I don't care."

Drew reached over and touched her shoulder. "God, you're uptight."

She shook off his touch. "I may be uptight, but I'm not stupid."

Something in his eyes turned savage.

"Take me home."

Her words hit like a strap across raw flesh. His flesh. He flinched.

"I want to go now." A tear crawled down her right cheek.

"With pleasure," he said in a low, terse voice.

Fourteen

―――

"They're too short," the woman wailed, and glared at Ann.

Ann prayed for patience. "But, Jessica, you sat here and told me to cut them off."

"But not completely," Jessica countered huffily.

"I had no choice. To make them look decent, I had to even them up, and that meant taking the majority of the length." Ann forced a smile. "They look lovely. Really they do."

"Well, I guess they do at that." Jessica's pained features relaxed. "How much do I owe you? I've got to get home. Elmer's going to kill me as it is."

Ten minutes later Ann was alone. She wilted against her chair and rubbed her right temple. A dilly of a headache was coming on. Jessica was typical of her day. She looked at the time. Six o'clock and she was just now finishing. Or just about. She still had to ready the shop for the next day.

On the other hand, she had no reason to hurry home. Nothing waited for her there except emptiness, the same emptiness she carried inside her. She had existed in a kind of limbo since her verbal skirmish with Drew.

She feared their relationship was severed for good. So face that and let it go, she told herself fiercely, getting up and stomping to the closet to get a broom. Let *him* go.

The harder she swept, the harder her mind worked. It was for the best that he'd swept out of her life, the same as he'd swept into it. But she missed him. Dear Lord, did she ever.

A week had passed since he'd pulled into her driveway after they'd ridden home in stony silence from the outing that had started with such sweet promise.

Scuttlebutt had it that he'd gone back to Houston to race. Ann leaned on the broom and felt a shudder pass through her. What if he had a wreck. . . . No! She wouldn't allow herself to think about that. But she couldn't control her thoughts; they ran rampant down that forbidden track. If the way Drew drove was an indicator, Drew wasn't afraid of the devil himself.

Another shudder shook her, as she remembered the Jag's hair-raising speed and the sick fear that had soured her stomach. She never wanted to experience anything like that again. But that was what Drew craved, that dangerous excitement, that living on the edge.

White-faced, Ann moved to the closet and replaced the broom. How could she have fallen in love with him? How could she have been so reckless?

Ann had counted on love, if it ever happened to her, to evolve slowly, to invade her heart quietly, with little or no fanfare. She had likened love to a tiny seed that must be watered and fed in order to grow and mature. She had always scoffed at the notion of bells and fireworks going off as a result of a look, a touch. No longer—having experienced exactly what she'd ridiculed. But never in her wildest imagination had she expected love to dominate her mind and senses to such a degree that everything else took second place.

Possessed.

That said it all. But even that failed to describe the churning inside her, the need that controlled her every thought, her every move. And the internal void was more noticeable than before.

With an effort, Ann held the tears at bay and finished her tasks. Then loaded down with her tote bag and purse, she walked to the door. The phone rang.

"Damn," she muttered, only to feel her heart leap. Maybe it was Drew....

She dropped her burden and hurried to the phone. When she lifted the receiver, she didn't know which pounded louder, her heart or her head.

"H-hello," she stammered.

"Ann, is that you?"

While she was disappointed that the caller wasn't Drew, she was thrilled that it was Dorothy Sable from the adoption agency.

"Did I catch you at a bad time?"

"No, of course not," Ann said hastily. "I was just about to go home."

"Would you rather I call you there?"

"Heavens, no."

"Well, this will only take a minute."

"It's always a pleasure hearing from you," Ann said, and grabbed the edge of the manicure table to steady herself.

"What I'm calling about," Dorothy said, "is to ask if you'd be willing to take an older child, a two-year-old for example? I know you'd prefer a newborn, but as we told you up front, they are almost always reserved for couples."

"And I told you I'd take my chances and wait."

"Correct. Do you still feel that strongly?"

Ann didn't hesitate. "No, no I don't. I'll be willing to take an older child, especially if it'll speed up the process."

"I can't promise that, of course, but it'll certainly help."

Red tape, Ann thought, tons and tons of red tape and more to look forward to. But then that was part and parcel of dealing with the state. Ridiculous, that was what it was. Yet she had no choice. She had to play by their rules or not at all.

"Ann?"

She heard the question in Dorothy's tone. "That's fine. Really it is."

"Good, then, I'll be in touch."

Once the receiver was back on the hook, Ann released her grip on the table and sank into a chair. She was thrilled, of course, and ached to share her good news with Drew. A grimace tightened her lips as she axed that thought. First, he couldn't care less; he thought she was crazy for wanting to adopt a child. And second, she doubted she'd see him again except in passing.

Maybe if she hadn't reacted so violently to his fast driving, tempered her fear... No! She couldn't hide her feelings. If she was happy, her friends knew it. If she was upset, they knew that, too. Like it or not, she had to be herself.

Ann switched off the light and went out the door, feeling more alone than she ever had in her life.

"You didn't hear a damn thing I said, did you?"

Drew raised sheepish eyes to stare at Hal Ackerman, his accountant friend. Instead of sitting at his massive desk, Hal leaned on a filing cabinet behind it and returned Drew's stare. Grim humor straightened his full lips.

"No, I didn't," Drew admitted bluntly.

Hal rubbed his protruding stomach. "It's clients like you who give me heartburn."

"Not hardly. It's all that greasy food you put away that does that."

To label Hal overweight was an understatement. Drew bet he tipped the scales at two-ninety. But his physical malady had no bearing, thank goodness, on his mind. It was as sharp as Drew remembered.

"You wanna discuss this another day?" Hal asked.

Drew squirmed in his chair, uncomfortable under Hal's intense scrutiny.

"No, dammit. I made a trip to Houston just to see you."

"I don't know what it is, but something's got hold of you and is chewing on you real good."

"Mind your own business, okay?"

Hal grinned. "You haven't changed a bit."

"Neither have you."

Although they didn't see each other often and had gone their separate ways out of high school and college, they had once been good friends and knew each other well enough to take certain liberties.

Hal laughed. "Somehow I don't think that's a compliment."

Drew snorted.

"It's got to be a woman," Hal said, his laughter deepening. "Always is."

Drew had no comeback, because Hal was right. This past week without Ann had been hell. He'd thought about little else. The more he'd cursed himself for his lack of control, the worse he'd felt. His need for her was so strong it had the potential to become an obsession. Up until now, he'd taken racing seriously, never a woman. Ann was certainly playing havoc with the order of his life.

"Yeah, it's a woman, all right. I can tell by the look on your face."

"Lay off, Ackerman," Drew warned, though his gruffness had a soft edge.

"Suit yourself."

"So what were you saying?" Drew asked, all business now.

"I was asking if you'd checked Pollard's bank account to make sure he hadn't built up a surplus?"

"Other than the fact that he's messing around with the teller, I found nothing out of the ordinary."

Hal yanked at his mustache. "He's putting the cash somewhere, and two will get you five that that sweet darlin' at the bank is obliging him in more ways than one."

Drew shot straight up. "You mean you found something?"

Hal patted himself on the back. "Yep."

"I'll be damned. Then I was right, the SOB is guilty."

"Guilty as sin, most likely."

"How's he doing it?"

Hal pushed away from the filing cabinet and crossed to his desk. "Invoices," he said, pointing toward the boxes lining the walls that Drew had carted there.

"So when can I go to the authorities?"

"Soon," Hal replied. "I'm still loading my guns, so to speak."

"Just say when," Drew said, and got to his feet, then headed for the door.

"Where're you off to in such a hurry?"

Drew stopped midstride and turned around. "Back to MacMillan. I've got some pressing, unfinished business I need to take care of."

"Wouldn't have anything to do with the woman, now would it?"

"When did you get to be such a nosy bastard, anyway?"

Hal's belly laugh rang in Drew's ear all the way down the hall.

"I'm coming. I'm coming."

Despite the door bell's insistent ring, Ann paused and stared briefly into the mirror on the wall. She bared her teeth, determined to make sure there was no grain of pepper lodged between them. She had just swallowed the last of a boiled egg.

Satisfied that none was there, she reached for the door and opened it. Drew's tall, imposing figure faced her. Ann's tongue clung to the dry roof of her mouth. She couldn't say anything nor could she move. Surprise robbed her of both functions.

"Can I come in?"

Was she mistaken or had his voice sounded unsteady? "Of...course," she said, stepping aside. She leaned against the door for support when he walked past her. His cologne swamped her senses, made her weak. He looked so good, and she was so glad to see him she would forgive him almost anything.

"I figured you'd tell me to go to hell," he said. They stood in the middle of the room, an arm's length apart.

"I'm not in the habit of telling people to do that."

He smiled, though it lasted only a second. "No, I guess not."

A short silence intruded.

"Why are you here?" she asked. Her voice sounded rusty.

"To apologize." His eyes delved into hers. "Again."

Ann tried to pull her gaze away, but couldn't. "Look—"

"I know what you're thinking," he said, a muscle twitching in his jaw. "I'm a real bastard and don't deserve another chance."

"I—"

"Let me finish. You're right, I am. And while I'm not sure I can change that, I'm willing to try." He shoved his hand through hair that needed a trim. "I don't know what the hell's happening between us—" he broke off and looked at her through tortured eyes "—but I don't want to stop seeing you."

He seemed to droop visibly, as if that long speech had exhausted him. Yet he didn't take his eyes off her.

"I . . . don't want to stop seeing you, either." Ann's heart sang inside her chest.

"Then come here," he muttered thickly.

With a cry that was both laughter and sobs, Ann ran headlong into his arms.

Fifteen

"It was so nice of you to keep me company, dear."

Janet MacMillan's soft voice sounded weak—though it was stronger than it had been two days ago when she'd been rushed to the hospital.

"The pleasure's mine," Ann said. She reached for the delicately veined hand and held it. "My...mother thought so much of you."

"No more than I thought of her. She was a fine lady."

"Thanks." Ann turned away. She feared Janet would see the tears that sprang into her eyes.

"So you and my son have been seeing a lot of each other." It was a statement, not a question.

Ann swung around and felt color steal into her face. "Mmm, that's right."

Janet squeezed Ann's hand. "Good. He needs a steadying influence."

Ann laughed. "Think so?"

"I know so. That son of mine thrives on danger. And speaking of my son, when is he due back?"

Ann glanced at her watch. "Anytime now, actually."

"I hope the doctor tells him he can take me home," Janet said, her eyes fluttering shut.

Ann disengaged her hand, then eased back into her chair. She had her doubts about Janet's release, for today anyway. When Drew finished at his office, he would have to tell his mother that the doctor preferred she remain another night.

Ann had been working late at the shop when Drew called and asked if she'd meet him at the emergency room. As soon as she'd hustled her last customer out the door, she'd driven to the hospital in Lufkin. A grim-faced Drew had met her at the entrance. His mother had had another attack, and while not critical, she was in pain.

She and Drew had waited for the doctor, hands locked tightly, which was something they had done a lot of the past two weeks. Following his apology for his recklessness in the car, they had been inseparable, especially during the evenings when they would play tennis or jog together, then drive to Lufkin to dine. But the majority of their time had been spent in each other's arms making love.

He only had to come near her and she would melt. But though the physical attraction was a heady part of their burgeoning relationship, it wasn't all. She loved his laughter and yes, his arrogant charm.

Drew, however, had never once told her he loved her; and she had convinced herself that he did. She'd also convinced herself that despite their differences, they had a future.

No one could be that attentive, that loving, if love wasn't the motivator. Or was she fooling herself, hoping for a miracle that might not happen? No. He had to love her. He just had to.

Now, as she heard the door open, she twisted around. Drew smiled before easing himself cautiously to the bed and mouthing, "Is she all right?"

Ann nodded, glad she was sitting down. Just looking at him made her go weak in the knees. He looked sensational, as usual, in black jeans and a white shirt that called attention to his tan and whipcord strength. She feared he could hear the thundering of her heart.

Janet's eyes opened. "I wasn't asleep."

Drew winked at Ann, then leaned down and kissed his mother on the cheek. "How're you feeling?"

"Fine. I'm ready to go home."

"Doc says maybe tomorrow."

Janet's face fell. "Talk to him, please. I know Kyle—he's known to change his mind quite often."

"Well, he knows what's best for you," Drew said soothingly. "So just don't ruffle the waters, okay? You scared the hell out of me as it was."

"Don't swear, Drew," she said primly.

His lips twitched as he looked at Ann. She hid a smile. "Yes, ma'am," he drawled.

"You two have something better to do than baby-sit me, I know. Anyway, I'm expecting Elizabeth any minute."

"Oh, Lord, let's get out of here, then," Drew said quickly, and reached for Ann's hand. "That ole biddy'll talk the horns off a billy goat and back on again."

"Drew MacMillan!"

"All right, I take that back." He leaned over and kissed her again. "We'll see you later."

"Take care, Mrs. MacMillan," Ann said softly, then followed Drew out the door.

The instant they got into the car, Drew reached for Ann and kissed her hard on the lips. "Mmm, you taste as good as you smell."

"I try," Ann said, when she recovered her breath.

"I've been dying to kiss you all afternoon."

"Same here."

He cranked the Jag and made his way onto the street.

"Where are we going?"

"To Mother's."

Ann raised her eyebrows. "We are?"

"Yep." He reached over and caressed a cheek. "Thought we'd grill steaks, jump in the hot tub, then make love till we can't walk."

"What if I'm not hungry?"

A red light caught them; he faced her with smoldering eyes. "I hope it's food you're talking about."

"As a matter of fact it is," she said, purposefully circling her lower lip with her tongue.

Drew sucked in his breath. "If you know what's good for you, you'll behave yourself."

Red tinted her face.

He chuckled. "I love it when you do that."

"I hate it," she said petulantly.

He laughed outright, then said, "So we'll skip the food and go straight to bed."

"You're insatiable."

"So are you."

She threw him a look.

"Only I'll admit it. The more I have of you, the more I want."

Ann's mouth went dry. "Same here."

They both fell silent.

"What about the housekeeper?" Ann asked at last.

Drew shifted positions. "Gave her the evening off."

"I don't know about you, Drew MacMillan."

"That's what keeps you coming back for more," he said arrogantly.

Ann laughed then was silent. She realized he was absolutely right—and that she loved him. But for now, the latter thought was her secret. No matter what the future held, the moment was hers. She wasn't about to waste a second of it.

"Drew, put me down. I'm too heavy."

"Like hell."

Ann giggled and sank closer against him while he climbed the stairs.

He had never felt so alive as he did when she was in his arms and he was inside her. Her fingernails scored his back while her moans rent the air. That high far surpassed anything he'd ever felt on the racetrack.

He hadn't thought he would ever find a woman who could make him feel that way. Admitting it, though, had a definite downside. It made him vulnerable and powerless—emotions he swore he'd never feel.

That was before Ann, before he'd sampled the delights of both her mind and her body, just as he was about to do again.

He reached his bedroom with haste and immediately stood her on her feet. Wordlessly, she stared at him, then placed a hand on his cheek.

Thunder clapped outside, and lightning danced around the sky. Neither could compare with what her gentle touch did to him. He shivered as he inhaled the warm, sweet smell of her. His need was so hot, so potent.

She unbuttoned his shirt, then slid her hand across his chest, sending another current through him.

He folded her against him and felt himself harden. He kissed her greedily and whispered, "I want you. I want you so much it's tearing me to pieces."

With trembling hands, he finished undressing her. She returned the favor with an excited awkwardness that was both sensuous and titillating.

"Love me," she said urgently, fitting her body to his as smoothly as the pieces of a puzzle. He embedded his fingers in her hair and sank his lips onto hers. They fell across the bed, their limbs tangled.

"I'm on fire," she whispered.

"And I ache."

He heard her whimper as he stroked her breasts with his tongue, then moved down her flat, smooth belly to the moistness between her thighs.

Minutes later, she placed her hands on either side of his head and pleaded in an agonized whisper, "Please, it's my turn."

He didn't have the willpower or the desire to refuse her. Her mouth, her lips and tongue were every bit as persuasive and primal as his in her effort to please. He heard himself moan and slip toward that edge, no longer in control.

"I want you," she pleaded. "I need you now!"

He entered her, and she cried out, her body shifting to accommodate his. He slid all the way up her. His own release came almost instantly, and then he heard her murmuring softly in sync with his own body's rocking movements.

He held onto her, reluctant to let go, as if she might be a delicious dream that would disappear. She sighed and squirmed closer. He touched her hair, her face, her lips with his fingers, determined to memorize each delicate feature.

"Was I too fast?" he asked, his breath fanning her cheek.

"No. You were perfect."

"Will I ever get enough of you?"

Ann made a tiny little sound in her throat. "I . . . hope not."

"You always smell good. What's the name of your perfume? I aim to keep you well supplied."

"It's Red Door."

"Hey, I'm serious."

"That's the name. Honest," she said.

"Helluva name for a fragrance, is all I can say." He slapped her playfully on her bottom.

"Ouch!"

"Ouch! You've got to be kidding. That didn't hurt."

"Wanna bet. Turn over and let me do the same to you—then we'll see."

He leaned over and tweaked a nipple. "I've got a better idea. Come on."

"Where're we going?" she asked, giving into the tug of his hand.

"You'll see."

They climbed together into the tub filled with hot, churning water, they faced each other, their legs entwined.

"God, this feels good."

"Mmm, it does, doesn't it?" Ann echoed his sentiments.

"But not as good as you." His lips closed over hers.

Ann moaned.

The phone rang. Their bodies tensed, then broke apart.

"Damn!" he cursed.

Ann giggled.

"I'd say to hell with it," he said, standing, "but I'm afraid it may be the hospital."

She purposely batted her lashes. "Don't worry, I'm not going anywhere."

He flashed her a hot glance, then climbed out of the tub.

When he returned, his features appeared cast in stone.

"Your mother?" she asked, frowning.

"No. It was the sheriff's office. They picked up Peter."

The officer, Mickey Hargrove, whom both she and Drew knew from their high school days, shoved his wide-brimmed hat farther back on his head and eyed Ann. "He admitted he broke into your shop."

Ann shuddered. Drew cursed.

During the ride to the station, she'd sat stoically beside Drew. Her heart had lain like a lump of lead in her chest, just the opposite of how she'd felt only minutes prior when she'd anticipated a romp in the water with Drew. Her comedown had been like a slap in the face, convincing her that no matter how hard she wanted to, she couldn't escape reality. And her brother was definitely reality. The cold, harsh kind.

Peter, she'd learned from Drew, had been picked up at a woman's house on the outskirts of town.

"Uh, what do you want to do, about pressing charges, I mean?" Mickey asked.

Ann shook her head. Drew had asked her that same question; she hadn't known the answer then, nor did she now.

"I'd like to see him first."

"Sure."

"Is . . . is he all right?"

"He is now. He was a sight for sore eyes, but I made him clean up." Mickey nodded toward a room off the main one. "He's in there."

"Thanks, Mickey," Ann said. Still, she hesitated.

"I'll go with you, if you want me to." Drew's hand circled her elbow.

She flashed him a watery, grateful smile, even though she knew his presence would exacerbate the situation. But she needed his support.

Peter sat slumped in a chair; his head was bent, resting on his hands. When he heard the sound of scuffling feet, he jerked his head up.

Ann held her breath and waited for him to curse her and create a scene because Drew was with her. He did neither. Instead, his dull eyes rested on them, then he turned away, his face pale and gaunt.

Ann's heart turned over. So much potential, so much waste. If only things had been different. They weren't, though, and she had to face the untenable situation head-on.

She ventured closer to Peter and forced herself to ask, "Why, Peter, why?"

He looked at her, his features contorted. "You wouldn't help me."

"And that was your way of paying me back?"

"Something like that."

Ann fought back the tears. "You ... you must hate me...."

"Sis ... please." Peter drew a deep breath. "Are ... are you going to press charges?"

"Do you think I should?"

"Yes," he said simply.

Drew stepped closer but remained silent.

Again Ann felt his strength and was grateful for it. "You're right, I should. Only I'm not going to."

Peter stared at her as if he hadn't heard her correctly, then his shoulders visibly relaxed. "Thank God," he croaked.

"But you're going to have to play by my rules." Ann's voice brooked no argument. "First, you're going to seek professional help."

"And I know just the right person," Drew put in. "There's a counselor in Nacogdoches who's the best."

"Dammit, Drew, I don't need a shrink."

"Yes, you do," Ann cut in forcefully.

"You also need a job," Drew added. "I'm willing to put you to work at the lumberyard."

Ann's eyes sought Drew's, and for a second it was as if they were the only ones in the room. Her look expressed her heartfelt thanks.

But when she turned back to Peter again, she saw that his face had turned paler. Ann sensed he was choking on Drew's offer, but this time he had no alternative and he knew it.

"All right," he said without looking at either of them. "I'll do it your way."

"But that's not all, Peter."

Ann's soft, but still firm voice brought him back around. "Whaddaya mean?" Peter demanded.

"I mean that I expect you to pay for the damage you did to my shop. I may not be pressing charges, but you're not about to get off scot-free."

He nodded.

"Also, once a week, I expect you at the shop after work to clean it. I haven't hired a cleaning service. For now, you can fill that bill."

"Anything else?" Peter asked in a dull tone.

"No... that's all."

"Why don't you come back to the house and stay with me tonight?" Drew offered, relieving some of the tension in the room.

Peter shook his head. "Thanks, but I'll go back to Sandra's, where I was picked up."

"Let's get out of here, then," Drew said.

But no one moved—at least not Ann or Peter. They stared at each other for a long moment, then Peter said in a pain-filled voice, "Sis... I'm... sorry."

"Oh, Peter," she whispered, crossing the room straight to his arms. "It's going to be all right. You'll see."

A short time later, Drew walked Ann to her door. He reached out and tipped her chin. Their eyes locked. "You sure you don't want me to stay with you?"

"No," she said huskily. "I think I need to be alone."

"You sure?"

She smiled against his hard chest. "Yes, I'm sure. Anyway, we both could use a good night's sleep."

He chuckled. "Touché."

"Call me."

"That goes without saying."

He kissed her then, and she clung to him for a minute. When they pulled apart, Drew said, "I have a favor to ask."

"Anything."

"I'm racing this weekend. Will you come and watch me?"

Ann forced herself not to react outwardly, though her heart wrenched. Was this a test? Somehow she thought it was. So she had to try. She loved him. Wasn't that reason enough to lend her support to something that was so important to him?

"Yes," she whispered, backing out of his arms and staring at him. "I'll come."

Sixteen

"By the way, did I tell you you look good enough to eat?"

Ann cut her eyes at Drew, who had one hand on the Jag's steering wheel and the other on her knee. She placed her hand over his; their fingers curled together. "No," she said, "but it's always nice to hear."

And it was, especially as she'd chosen her clothes carefully this morning. She knew the red cotton jumpsuit with white piping trim was a perfect foil for her black hair and alabaster skin. White sandals, silver earrings and a bracelet completed the outfit.

The day of the race finally arrived. In spite of her reservations, she was excited. That excitement stemmed from spending the entire day with Drew and partly from the news she was eager to share with him.

Since they had gone to the jail to confront her brother, so much had happened. Two days afterward, she and Drew had driven Peter to Nacogdoches to meet with the counselor. Ann had been impressed with the tall, clear-spoken doctor. His overall manner depicted complete confidence in his ability to help someone like Peter. Once the sessions had begun and Peter attended in good faith, Drew put him to work at the lumberyard.

Though still concerned for her brother's well-being, Ann had tried to put things in perspective. The call from the adoption agency had certainly helped. Her first home visit was scheduled for next week. She'd found it hard not to blurt out the news to Drew, if for no other reason than to test his reaction.

But she hadn't. She planned to tell him tonight, after the race, when they were snuggled in bed.

She studied him. As usual, she felt a warm feeling invade her body. She loved him with her whole being, and with each passing day she was convinced he loved her, too. Soon he would say the words she longed to hear.

She averted her gaze to his racing gear. The flame-retardant suit seemed to mock her. Her stomach lurched. *Flame-retardant.* The words and their meaning weighed heavy on her heart. No, she told herself. No gloomy thoughts today.

Drew looked at her and said, ''What's wrong?''

''Wrong?''

''Yeah, wrong.'' He frowned. ''You looked like you just thought of something distasteful.''

She made herself smile. ''Didn't mean to.''

He kept his eyes on her another minute, as if he wanted to take issue, but he didn't. Instead, he crooked his head so as to peer at the sky. "I'm holding my breath the bottom won't fall out."

Ann also craned her neck. "How can you even think that when there's not a cloud in the sky?"

"Hell, in East Texas anything can happen."

"True, but you've got to think positive."

He gave her a self-conscious shrug. "Nerves, I guess."

"You're nervous?" Ann teased. "I don't believe it."

"Well, believe it," he said flatly, only to smile then. "But it's a good kind of nerves, gets the adrenaline flowing."

"Do you realize I know zilch about racing?"

"Well," he drawled, "that's because you've never asked."

"I'm asking now. So tell me."

"My car is what you call a top-fuel dragster. It has a long snout in front, and the rear is a miniature airplane wing."

"Sounds like something out of *Star Wars.*"

He flashed her an indulgent smile. "It's flashier, actually."

"Figures," she said ruefully.

He laughed.

"How fast will it go?"

"Are you sure you want to know?"

Ann's face clouded. "No, but if you don't tell me, I'll imagine it's worse than it really is."

"It travels over two hundred and fifty miles per hour."

"Oh, my. I wish you hadn't told me," Ann said with a small voice, battling a sick feeling in her stomach.

"Are you all right? You've got that funny color again."

Ann straightened and forced a lightness into her tone. "I'm fine."

"And pigs fly."

She gave him a scathing glance. "So I guess you sit practically on top of the engine. I might as well get all the bad stuff in one lump sum."

"It sits right behind me, all right, but I'm cocooned in the cage."

"Cage?"

"Cockpit. And by the way, the starting line is called Christmas tree."

"That's weird."

He chuckled. "I thought you'd get a kick out of that."

"All this is carefully regulated, isn't it?" she asked anxiously.

"You bet. The National Hot Rod Association is the sanctioning organization that makes the rules and makes sure we abide by them."

"That's good to know."

He reached over and again trapped her hand in his. He brought it to his lips. Shivers danced down her spine. Only one look, one touch, and she went off inside like a firecracker.

"You're going to love it," he said with an answering light in his eyes. "I suspect you're going to like it so much that you'll want to watch again."

"Tacky, tacky."

He dropped her hand at the same time a belly laugh tensed his stomach.

She reached over and yanked his ear in retaliation.

"Remind me to pay you back for that." His eyes honed in on her. "Later."

"Is that a promise?" She barely recognized her voice.

"Count on it."

They finished the trip wrapped in a cloak of warm euphoria. Only after Drew pulled into the racetrack parking lot in Baytown a short time later did the silence break.

"Do I get a kiss for luck?" he asked hoarsely, running his eyes over her.

"Oh, Drew," she whispered, and dove into his arms. "Please, please be careful."

The sun sparkled in the sky like a huge jewel. Perched on the bleachers among thousands of cheering, flag-waving fans, Ann waved her banner and clapped with the crowd. She eyed the track and was shocked. Drew hadn't told her it was only a quarter of a mile in distance or that it was straight, not a circle as she'd thought. But then she hadn't asked him about it, apparently he'd assumed she knew.

The announcer came on the loudspeaker and named the cars and their positions. When Drew's was called, she again questioned the sanity of what she was doing.

A day after she'd told him she would watch him race, she'd been traumatized with fear. How could she sit and watch him blatantly endanger his life? She hadn't known the answer then, and she didn't know it now. Nevertheless, here she was, mingling with the jubilant crowd, determined to fulfill her promise no matter what the cost to her peace of mind.

Drew knew what he was doing, didn't he? And it was only one race, for Pete's sake. She would soon ridicule herself for her foolishness. Meanwhile, she would hold close the thought that Drew was a professional. And pray.

Two cars took their position—Drew's and one other. She chanted, "Drew, Drew," along with the crowd. Her man was a favorite.

Ann felt the tension and the excitement mount. She had absolutely no saliva left in her mouth.

"Ladies and gentlemen," the announcer cried over the loudspeaker, "are you ready?"

"Yes," the crowd screamed in response.

Since both men had an outside lane, neither had the advantage. But Ann felt sure that wouldn't make any difference to Drew. She had a clear view of him, and that was what counted. She locked her eyes on Drew's brightly painted dragster and waited, her heart in her throat.

"Start your engines!"

The flag shot up. The gun boomed. Ann watched as Drew wrapped his hands around the steering wheel and nailed the pedal.

Suddenly, brutally, his engine exploded in flames.

Drew!

Ann bolted out of her seat and tried to scream, but raw fear closed her throat. She could only stand and

stare in horror. The pit crew stampeded toward him.
The fire fighters and the medical crew did, too. Waves
of fear washed over her, leaving her body paralyzed.

Was he dead? Dear Lord, *no!* She saw him then, not
being lifted onto a stretcher, but climbing out of the
cockpit on his own volition.

"Thank God," Ann whispered.

The crowd roared and whistled in relief while two
men got on either side of Drew and, after lifting him,
carried him toward the pit.

With tears blinding her, Ann felt for the chair behind her, positive she was going to faint.

She must have cried out because the man next to her
dropped back into his seat and stared at Ann. "Lady,
you all right?"

Ann couldn't say a word. She took deep gulping
breaths and tried to regain control. The frozen feeling
in her heart, the building pressure in her stomach, her
limbs shaking as if she had the palsy, and the rank
taste in her mouth were all standard symptoms of
panic.

"Lady, answer me!"

"Please," she whispered through bloodless lips,
"take me to the man who...who was hurt."

"You with him?"

Ann could only nod.

"Jeez, come on, then, I'll see what I can do."

Ann never knew how she found Drew or how she
ended up alone with him in a cubbyhole in the make-
shift infirmary. She thought his pit-crew manager had
probably intercepted her and taken charge. She just

knew that she now stood across from Drew, her eyes taking in the scratch on his forehead and the extreme pallor of his skin.

Yet, he was smiling as he came toward her. "Sorry, I didn't make a better impression. That's what I get for wanting to show off. Maybe next time I won't screw up." He reached for her.

She slapped at his hands and stepped back.

"Ann...?"

"Don't...don't you dare touch me!"

A hard shudder raked him. "For god's sake, don't look at me like that. See, I'm fine. Just a mild concussion."

"Oh, is that all?" She laughed, only it came out a sob. "Just a mild concussion! How...how can you toss that off as nothing?" She heard her voice rise with each word, approach the level of hysteria, but she didn't care. "Damn you! You...you could've been killed. And for what!"

"Hey, take it easy. You're blowing this way out of proportion."

"Oh, really. Oh, that's great. Well, I happen to have been there and watched while your car blew up."

"Well, *I* happened to have been in the car, and it's no big deal. Accidents come with the territory."

The terror that Ann had experienced earlier was nothing compared to what she felt now. Outrage and shock and disbelief. An excruciating pain ripped through her insides. She feared she would throw up on the spot. How in the name of God could he treat a near-miss on his life so lightly?

"You can't handle it, can you?" His voice sounded as if the life had gone out of it.

"No, I guess I can't."

"Can't or don't want to?"

His penetrating blue eyes seemed to read her soul. She steeled herself against their magnetic pull for understanding. "Maybe a little of both."

"I see."

"No, I don't think you do."

A muscle in Drew's cheek throbbed. "If I thought something like this would've happened, I would never have insisted you come. But since we can't predict the future, you'll have to accept what happens and go on. The way I see it, life's one big gamble, anyway."

"Not to me it isn't."

Drew smiled a cold smile. "You're right about that. If it's not a sure thing, you aren't interested, right?"

"What I think or feel isn't the issue here," she said.

"Oh, but it is. You know the word that best describes you is *coward*. You're a coward, Ann Sinclair."

"That's not true!" she countered.

"Yes, it is. The thought of taking a chance absolutely blows your mind." His eyes were stormy. "The bottom line here is, you're afraid."

A warning went off in her brain. But she refused to heed it. She had to say the words crowding her throat or choke on them. "I'm not afraid of taking chances that count," she threw back at him. "Such as commitments to the important things in life."

The silence that followed was stark. Both were trapped in the fragility of the moment. Every word, every gesture, every sensation became important, threatening.

"It's not going to work, is it?" Drew said in an emotionless voice.

Ann's pulse pounded in her ears. "Not if you don't want it to," she whispered.

Tension stiffened his jaw, and he didn't say anything.

Something cold settled in the bottom of her stomach. "Oh, I want it to, all right," she said, feeling herself break apart inside, "but I'm greedy. I want it all—a home, children, but most of all a husband who's a man and not a spoiled little boy with a penchant for danger."

Drew's face crumpled, then twisted bitterly. "In that case, I guess you'd best hightail it back to that safe, boring world where *change* and *excitement* are dirty words. Personally, I no longer give a damn."

Ann reeled.

"I'll have my manager drive you home."

The abrupt slam of the door rocked the trailer.

The fear, the sickness she'd felt before in no way rivaled the blinding agony that bent her double.

Was it over? Was *he* over? Bile stuck in Ann's throat as she stood transfixed and watched her dreams, her hopes, disintegrate. You always did want what you couldn't have, a voice taunted.

"No...!" Another agonizing pain ripped through her.

Seventeen

"**Y**ou sure you aren't sick?"

Drew was sick all right, but he wasn't about to admit it. He glowered at his assistant. "Hell, no. I already told you that."

"So you did." Skip scratched his head. "Something's got you riled, that's for sure." He paused. "It's not your mother, is it?"

Drew's features relaxed somewhat. "No. For the time being, she's doing okay."

"That's good news. I also have some more good news."

"Shoot."

"If you still want the property, it's yours."

"I want it," Drew said without much enthusiasm, which garnered another strange look from Skip. He ignored it and went on, "Go ahead and start the paperwork rolling."

"Right." Skip walked toward the door. "Oh, I almost forgot, Hal Ackerman called and said he was on his way here."

"'Bout damn time," Drew muttered. "Tell Wendy I'll see him immediately."

Alone, Drew stood and walked to the window, his stride jerky, like that of an old man. He cursed himself, and while he had the urge to shove his hand through the plate-glass window, he didn't. Resorting to unnecessary violence was not the answer to his stupidity.

He'd told Ann he didn't give a damn. A sneer stretched his lips. Famous last words. He gave a damn, all right, only he hadn't recognized that until it was too late.

Though he kept the highway hot between Mac-Millan and Houston, he spent the majority of his time here at the office. He felt he could cope better. Besides, his dealerships had gone without his attention long enough. Since his mother was doing as well as could be expected, and he'd gotten his daddy's business better organized, except for the Tim Pollard debacle, he'd felt free to concentrate on his own bailiwick.

Or so he'd thought. The lines deepened in his forehead at the same time the door opened behind him. He swung around and watched as the accountant waddled across the threshold.

"Your secretary told me to come on in," Hal said by way of a greeting.

"Want a cup of coffee?" Drew asked.

"Naw, just had one, but thanks, anyway." Hal's eyes narrowed on Drew. "You sick?"

An expletive scorched the air. "What is this? First Skip, now you. No, dammit, I'm not sick."

"Hey, I didn't mean anything by that." Hal's nonchalant smile seemed to lengthen his mustache. "It's just that you look godawful, like maybe you've been chasing the bottle."

"Give it a rest, okay?"

Hal shrugged. "Whatever you say."

"So tell me what you've come up with." Drew perched on the edge of his desk.

Hal shifted his massive body weight into action. He set his briefcase down. "I've got proof."

"Proof that'll nail his butt?"

"To the prison floor."

"Good."

"Is that all you can say?"

Drew raised his eyebrows as he stood. "What would you like for me to say?"

"How should I know," Hal said darkly. "Shout hallelujah, or better still, why not jump over the desk?" Hal's attempt at humor fell on deaf ears as Drew strode back to the window and stared outside. "Just show some emotion," Hal added.

How can you show emotion when you're dead inside? Drew wondered. Ann, sweet Ann. She was the best thing that had ever happened to him, and he had let her go.

He ached for her, ached to feel her naked against him, ached to kiss her beautiful belly, feel her breasts against his cheek, hear that purring sound that was all her own.

Her image surged to his mind with such vividness that it was all he could do to collect his thoughts and pay attention as the accountant walked over to him, a sheet full of figures in his hand.

"Here's the proof," Hal said.

Drew shook himself and faced Hal, though he felt vulnerable, exposed. "Were you right?"

"Yep. The receipts don't match the deposits."

"So the little weasel's been pocketing the money."

"With the help of his sweetie at the bank."

"Sonofagun!" For a moment Drew's eyes returned to life. "She's been depositing the money in her account."

"I'd stake just about anything on it," Hal responded.

"Let me make sure I got this straight. Pollard helps himself to the money, then adjusts the deposits accordingly. And because he was confident he'd never get caught, he didn't bother or didn't know how to adjust the cash-register tapes."

"I'd say that's it in a nutshell," Hal said.

Drew folded the paper and shoved it into his shirt pocket. "Anything else I need to take to the authorities?"

"That about covers it."

"I had confidence in you from the beginning, my friend."

"Why don't I think that's a compliment?" Hal asked at the door.

Drew actually smiled. "Well, it is. You did a helluva job. Thanks."

"As always," Hal said, and sauntered out the door.

Drew hadn't wanted to go home, but he had no other place to go. He'd gone the bar route, only booze hadn't helped to ease the yearning inside him. Rather, it had intensified it, made him less human.

It was twelve o'clock and raining like hell. He'd stayed at the office until he was so weary, he'd had trouble driving home.

But the instant he'd opened the door and walked inside, it had hit him, as he knew it would—the desperate hunger to see her, to hold her. Again, he longed to feel Ann's arms around him, feel her warm, seeking lips against his, feel the solidness of her body. The craving was so bad it gnawed in his gut, like a virus that kept lingering.

He trudged into the bedroom, stripped quickly and fell onto the bed. Nights tore him up. The loneliness was unbearable.

How could he have loved her and not known it? He guessed he'd fought so hard *not* to love her that he hadn't recognized the symptoms. He'd told himself that if she couldn't love him as he was, his goals and dreams included, then a relationship between them was doomed. And it was better to know that now than later.

This way he could start to rebuild his life. He still had what was important to him—his work and his love of racing. He would be fine.

Only he wasn't. He was miserable.

He loved her so much that his life had changed. Where once it had been challenging and exciting to wake up, now it was a drag. The color had gone out of everything. He missed her so much that his whole body throbbed.

"Ann," he said, his face against the pillow. "Ann."

He rolled back over, squeezed his eyes shut and gave in to the pain of losing her. He thought again about how she'd said, "I'm not afraid of taking chances that count. Such as commitments to the important things in life." He knew then, with the certainty of death and taxes, that he couldn't go on like this. He had to have her back.

She should be celebrating, Ann told herself. Her life, as she'd planned it, was exactly on course. Unfortunately, the course had changed. When she'd first mapped it out, Drew hadn't been a part of it.

She'd planned to expand her shop, employ a beautician and add a skin-care line, which she had firmed up just three days ago. And while she hadn't planned on her brother's reappearance, she was glad, especially as he'd responded to counseling and made a conscientious effort to become a responsible citizen.

But the enthusiasm was gone; the joy of accomplishment was missing. When Drew went out of her life, a light switched off inside her, plunged her into the dark—a dark from which she couldn't seem to emerge.

Even now as she waited for Dorothy Sable to pull out of her briefcase a raft of papers that needed signing, Ann felt that darkness taunt her with its menacing presence. Yet, she wanted this child, maybe more than before. It had become her lifeline; it was all she had left—the thought of someone to love, and to love her.

Still, a child wouldn't completely alleviate the dark void inside her. Only Drew could do that. Dear Lord, had it been only three weeks since they had parted? It seemed more like three years. She couldn't remember the last time she'd slept through the night.

Dreams wreaked havoc with her sleep. Often they were colorful, sexual dreams about Drew. Sometimes she awoke, sat straight up in bed, panting and clammy with perspiration, positive he was beside her, only to be devastated to find that he wasn't. Her overactive mind took its toll on her body.

Sophie had summed it up quite adequately. "If you don't start eating, you're going to dry up and blow away. You look like a walking corpse."

"I'm trying, really I am," Ann said.

"Pooh, you're not, either." Sophie fell silent a moment, then added, "Look, I know you're having a tough time since Drew...but you can't keep your feelings bottled inside forever."

"I know," Ann said through a haze of tears. "Just bear with me a while longer, okay?"

"If you want a shoulder—" Sophie paused and patted hers "—you got one."

"Thanks, I'll keep that in mind."

That conversation had taken place right after the breakup and still, Ann couldn't bring herself to open her heart and bleed on anyone, not even to Sophie.

"Ann?"

She breathed deeply, and forcing a smile, turned around. "Sorry. My mind was wandering."

"You seem upset." Dorothy looked concerned. "Is there something I should know about?"

"No," Ann assured her hastily, and smiled harder. "Pressures at work, you know," she finished lamely, praying that Dorothy wouldn't question her further.

Dorothy didn't. She returned Ann's smile and said, "It's a good thing you have your work. So many women who are waiting for a child don't have anything to occupy them."

"While I might not have that problem," Ann said softly, "the waiting is still nerve-racking."

"I know, and we're sorry. Unfortunately, the time factor remains the biggest drawback for adoptions."

"How long will I have to wait?"

Dorothy rose, her eyes sympathetic. "I wish I could say we would have a child for you anywhere from a year or two years. Or six months from now."

"The latter's not very likely, though, is it?" Ann asked wistfully.

"No, but it's not impossible, either. So, let's hold on to that thought, shall we?"

Ann nodded as she walked her guest to the door.

Dorothy extended her hand. "Take care, and I'll be in touch."

Rain slapped against the window. Ann tossed back the cover and got out of bed. But she didn't feel rested. As usual, she hadn't slept. She padded to the window, opened the miniblinds and stared at the sky.

Lightning streaked across it, then left only darkness in its wake, the same darkness that had set up permanent residence in her soul. With a sigh, she turned away from the window and eyed the bed. Today was Monday and she didn't have to work. But returning to bed was futile.

If only she had her child. That wasn't the answer, and she knew it. Only Drew could fill the emptiness in her life. So what was the answer? Certainly not surrounding herself in self-pity.

Again their bitter exchange rose to haunt her. Lord knows, she'd thought of little else.

Was Drew right? Was she a coward? Absolutely not. She was willing to gamble on single parenthood. Why, then, hadn't she given their relationship a chance? Was it because she feared she couldn't live up to his expectations, satisfy him? But if she didn't try, how would she know? She wouldn't.

But the real question was whether she could accept him for what he was, not for what she wanted him to be. Her heart gave a decided lurch. She thought for a second she might be having a heart attack; no, it was her conscience.

Had she been wrong to try to change him? Like a fist to her stomach, the answer rang clear. Yes. His recklessness, his irreverence for the status quo, were the things that made him special, made her love him.

Shaking all over, Ann dashed to the closet. She knew what she had to do.

Eighteen

Yesterday's storm had passed. Sunlight spilled onto the pavement in front of the car and created a harsh glare as well as aggravating the insufferable humidity.

The back of Ann's blouse was damp. But her problem was nerves, not the weather. She inhaled cool air-conditioned air deep into her lungs, then lowered the window and killed the engine. A waft of soggy air slapped her in the face.

She shook. This would never do. Now that she was here, several yards from Drew's condo in southwest Houston, fear threatened to render her useless.

Her watch said seven o'clock. She'd gotten off to a later start than she'd anticipated. Her plans had gone astray. She'd had two appointments she'd wanted to cancel but hadn't because both clients spent a lot of money in the shop every week.

Too, she'd gone by the dealership, thinking she might find him there, only to learn that he was at home nursing a cold.

The neighborhood was quiet. And the condos that lined the drive were elegant. The air was rich with the smell of money. From where she parked, his condo filled her vision. It appeared deserted, but then so did all the others on the street.

She breathed deeply. Her heart was banging so badly, she couldn't move. She needed time to collect herself.

It wasn't that she didn't want to go through with confronting Drew. She had no choice. She didn't want to live another day without him. She might have to, though, and the reality rooted her to the seat. She didn't know what she would do if he rejected her.

While her stomach turned somersaults, she opened the door and got out. She stood beside the car and took another deep breath. Then she looked to make sure her blue silk shirt and slacks were not mussed. She wanted to look her best. So much was at stake.

By the time she reached the door, a calm had settled over her. What she was about to do was right; and that resolve gave her the strength to push the doorbell.

No response. Only silence greeted her.

She pushed the bell again.

Heavy footsteps finally reached her ears. She clasped one hand around her purse and waited.

The door swung back on its hinges, and Drew filled the empty space. New lines scored his face and accentuated its gauntness. And his body was leaner. But his eyes hadn't changed, except the devilish tinkle was no longer there.

"What..?" His words halted—as if someone had landed a suckerpunch to the gut. Disbelief settled over his face. And something else, something she couldn't decipher.

He set his lips in a rigid line, and Ann's body tensed. Oh, God, he wasn't glad to see her, she realized. She'd made a mistake. She felt herself dismantling inside piece by piece, and there wasn't anything she could do to stop it.

A pitiful moan escaped her lips, and she stepped back. That was when she saw it. The fixed control slipped from his features; naked misery took its place. Ann's steps faltered.

"Don't . . . go," he said in a gravelly voice. He held out his arms.

She launched herself into them and sobbed against his chest, "Oh, Drew, hold me."

He strained to bring her closer, savoring the moment, thinking maybe he'd died and gone to heaven.

"I love you, I love you," he whispered. "I was coming to tell you that, only I got sick."

Ann raised her face. "That's why *I'm* here. I love you, too, and couldn't stand the thought of living another day without you."

His mouth found hers with a tempered fury. "This isn't enough," he said frantically. "I want all of you. Now."

Ann wordlessly grabbed his hand and placed it on her breast. He led her to his bedroom.

With the late-afternoon sun barred from the room by the blinds, Ann and Drew roughly, quickly discarded their clothes. When the articles pooled at their feet, they reached for each other.

"Oh, God, I dreamed of this moment," he ground out against her lips. "But I didn't think it'd ever happen."

"I missed you so much, so much." Her voice held agony and ecstasy. Her eyes held promise.

"Marry me."

She made that purring sound he loved so much. "Just say when."

"Tomorrow."

"What about your mother?" Her eyes were closed, but her lips were curved sensuously.

His gentle, but impatient fingers plucked a nipple. "What about her?"

"Shouldn't...shouldn't we include her? And Sophie? And maybe Peter?"

His lips took small tender bites along her neck. "Only if tomorrow suits them."

Ann whimpered and leaned helplessly against him. "Why the hurry? I promise not to leave you." Her tongue moved down his chest in long strokes.

Her heat set him on fire.

"Not ever," she added, a tremor running through her.

"Anything you say," Drew said hoarsely, and dragged her backward onto the bed.

Her lips were hot and sure beneath his, parting so their tongues could entwine. Then, shifting within his arms, she flattened herself against him. He was so hard he hurt.

He couldn't wait. He had to have her now. He shifted, placing enough distance between them so that he could position himself above her.

But she stopped him with her hand. Her violet eyes glowed as her flawless naked body inched its way upward to cover his. Her moistness instantly enveloped his thickness. He struggled for breath. She smiled at him and brought her breasts close to his lips. He took one in his mouth, then the other.

"Ah, Drew, Drew," she said in a prolonged whisper, beginning to move. With each stroke, everything, especially the past, ceased to exist.

Ann awakened and tried to move. She couldn't. Her body was still tangled with his.

"Hey, you," she whispered, "wake up."

"Mmm, I'm awake."

She sought his face, her eyes luminous and huge. "Will you forgive me?"

"Whatever for?"

"For trying to change you. When you race, I ... I promise I'll be strong."

"Oh, baby, baby," he said, cradling her close to his chest and rocking her. "You're something else."

"I'd rather have you for one day than not at all."

"We'll have lots of days. Do you think I'd honestly do anything to jeopardize that?"

"I ... hope not."

"Count on it." Drew's eyes narrowed in sudden pain. "I'm the one who should be apologizing for being so pigheaded and unbending. Hell, anyone in his right mind would've reacted the same way you did."

"But I'll do better next time," she said.

"Just be yourself, honey."

"Even if I get upset?"

"Even if you get upset."

"Oh, Drew." Her lower lip trembled.

He tongued it again before whispering, "I love you."

"And I love you."

He held her for a long moment, then said, "If you want to leave the adoption application on file, I won't object."

Like spring rain on wild flowers, his words fell delicately into the silence. Ann hugged them close, then pulled back and sought his eyes. "Thanks for that. And I want you to know that I love you even more for having said it."

"So how 'bout we start making our own baby," he muttered thickly.

Tears clumped her lashes as she smiled a beautiful, radiant smile. "I can't think of anything I'd rather do," she whispered. He groaned and covered her body with his.

Epilogue

Ann decided that pinching herself wasn't the answer. But she was tempted, if only to prove that she was alive. And well. And pregnant.

I'm going to have a baby!

After leaving the doctor's office, she had gone straight home. That had been over an hour ago, and her feet hadn't touched the ground yet. But dogging the heels of her elation was apprehension. With only eight months of marriage to her credit, what would Drew's reaction be?

She hoped and prayed he'd be as happy as she was. She had no reason to suspect otherwise as their marriage was as close to perfect as it could be. Too, he'd told her he'd wanted to make a baby even before they were married.

A giddy, indulgent smile crossed her lips as the thought struck her that almost all newlyweds feel this way. But she knew she and Drew had something special.

From day one he'd made her blissfully happy, which was not to say there hadn't been disagreements and adjustments. There had. But because their love was strong, they had weathered them together.

Both their professional lives had remained on track, which accounted for part of their well-being. With Drew's help, she'd expanded her shop. Business couldn't have been better.

Drew continued to experience growth in his car dealerships, as well, though he'd turned over day-to-day management to his assistant.

And while he still raced, his desire had tempered somewhat as the family business continued to take up more of his time. With so much happening right in MacMillan, they had decided to stay.

Tim Pollard had confessed and was serving time in jail. When the news had broken, gossip was rampant, but soon the citizens had tired of that scandal and searched for another one.

Thank goodness, her brother hadn't been new fodder for the gossip mongers. Therapy had helped him tremendously. He worked every day and had paid off the loan shark. He was learning to feel good about himself.

Ann found she had very little to complain about. She coveted her happiness and felt she'd earned it. At this moment, she coveted it even more, knowing that a tiny life was growing inside her.

Suddenly noticing the time, Ann made a face. She had to get going. Still, she didn't move. Her gaze was locked on the snow-flecked Christmas tree that dominated one corner of the den of the MacMillan mansion where they lived.

Drew had wanted to build her a new home, but she'd opted to live here instead, at least for the time being. Besides, she loved the stately old home and its treasures, and took pleasure adding her stamp to them.

Two months into their marriage, Drew's mother had become completely bedridden and, with a live-in companion, occupied her own apartment in the rear.

The lights on the tree twinkled at Ann. She laughed aloud, then placed her hand on her stomach. A baby. What a delightful Christmas present.

Finally, Ann forced herself to move. Drew was expected home for lunch. Every Monday he came home at noon; the habit had developed into a special time for them. Sometimes they ate; sometimes they made love instead.

She scurried into the bedroom where she took off her clothes and slipped into a baggy pair of knit pants and a top.

A short time later, she stood at the kitchen cabinet preparing a salad and humming at the top of her lungs.

"Gotcha."

Her heart jumped, then settled when she felt familiar arms encircle her.

She leaned against Drew's chest and looked up at him. "Don't you know it's not nice to sneak up on people?"

He grinned and nuzzled her neck. "You're not people—you're my wife."

She twisted in his arms and faced him. "Somehow I fail to see the logic in that."

He leaned down and planted a hot, hard kiss on her lips. "Mmm, you taste delicious," he whispered when he pulled away.

Ann wrinkled her nose. "So do you."

That devilish glint appeared in his eyes. "How 'bout feasting on each other, then?"

Ann feigned shock. "The very idea. And miss out on my wonderful salad?" She laughed. "Not a chance. Anyway, I have something to tell you."

"Oh?" Drew turned her loose, leaned against the cabinet, crossed his arms and with caressing eyes, watched her.

Ann licked her dry lips. "I went to the doctor today."

He stood straighter. "And?"

"I'm . . . I'm pregnant."

A hush descended over the room.

"Are you sure?" His voice sounded scratchy.

"Yes," she said. "You . . . you aren't sorry, are you?"

"Sorry? Of course not, silly. I can't think of anything better than our child inside you."

"Oh, Drew," she cried, flinging her arms around his neck and squeezing him.

He lifted her and swung her around the room. She squealed in delight. Once he settled her back on her feet, he stared at her.

"Isn't there a certain matter you should take care of?"

She gave him a perplexed look. "What?"

"The adoption agency."

Ann's mouth fell open. "Gosh, you're right."

He chuckled. "Since we're going to have our own baby, you really ought to think about canceling your application."

"I—" The phone stopped her answer.

Drew groaned. "Great timing."

Ann laughed, then crossed to the phone. She lifted the receiver, winked at Drew, then placed her hand across her stomach.

Desire simmered in his eyes.

"Hello," Ann said, weak-kneed.

She listened, while the high color seeped from her face.

"Honey?" Drew said, stepping forward.

She covered the receiver with her hand. "It's...it's Dorothy Sable...."

Drew paled.

"She...she wants to know if we can come and get a two-year-old girl...says she's ours...if we want her."

Drew cleared his throat roughly. "Do we want her?"

"Do we?" Ann whispered, and stared at him, knowing her heart was in her eyes.

Drew grinned his brash, cocky grin. Two babies. Hell, what could be more perfect?"

* * * * *

SILHOUETTE® *Desire*™

COMING NEXT MONTH

#733 THE CASE OF THE MISSING SECRETARY—Diana Palmer
MOST WANTED
Logan Deverell disliked disruption of his orderly life. But when
secretary Kit Morris decided this bear had been left in hibernation too
long, suddenly calm turned to chaos!

#734 LOVE TEXAS STYLE!—Annette Broadrick
SONS OF TEXAS
Allison Alvarez didn't need any help raising her son, especially not
from rugged businessman Cole Callaway—the man who had turned
his back on her and her baby fifteen long years ago....

#735 DOUBLECROSS—Mary Maxwell
Secret agent Travis Cross was hunting a murderer. But while hiding
out with sexy schoolteacher Alexis Wright, he caught a case of the
chicken pox, and the prescription was love!

#736 HELD HOSTAGE—Jean Barrett
When timid Regan MacLeod was stranded in the snowy wilderness
with accused murderer Adam Fuller, she knew survival depended on
trusting the handsome, bitter man—that and body heat....

#737 UNTOUCHED BY MAN—Laura Leone
As far as scholarly Clowance Masterson was concerned,
Michael O'Grady was a disreputable swindler. But the more time they
spent together, the more she fell prey to his seductive charm....

#738 NAVARRONE—Helen R. Myers
September's *Man of the Month*, Navarrone Santee, had only one
priority—proving his longtime enemy was a brutal killer. But his
efforts were blocked by sultry Dr. Erin Hayes.

SILHOUETTE® Desire™

presents

SONS OF TEXAS
by Annette Broadrick

As rugged as their native land, the Callaway brothers—Cole, Cameron and Cody—are three sinfully sexy heroes ready to ride into your heart.

In September—
LOVE TEXAS STYLE! (SD#734)

In October—
COURTSHIP TEXAS STYLE! (SD#739)

In November—
MARRIAGE TEXAS STYLE! (SD#745)

Don't let these Sons of Texas get away—men as hot as the Texas sun they toil . . . and *romance* . . . under! Only from Silhouette Desire . . .

1

FREE
BOOK COUPON

IMPORTANT: SAVE THIS COUPON. SIX COUPONS ENTITLE YOU TO A FREE COPY OF SILHOUETTE'S KEEPSAKE EDITION OF THE *10TH ANNIVERSARY COLLECTION.*

SDBP-1A

1

FREE
BOOK COUPON

IMPORTANT: SAVE THIS COUPON. SIX COUPONS ENTITLE YOU TO A FREE COPY OF SILHOUETTE'S KEEPSAKE EDITION OF THE *10TH ANNIVERSARY COLLECTION.*

© 1990 HARLEQUIN ENTERPRISES LTD.

IT'S YOURS FREE!

10TH ANNIVERSARY COLLECTION

FREE BOOK COUPON

It's Silhouette Desire's 10th Anniversary and we'd like to give you a special gift! Save this free book coupon. Six coupons entitle you to receive a free copy of Silhouette Desire's *10th Anniversary Collection*, three classic novels of love and romance.

YOUR NAME

ADDRESS

CITY   STATE/PROV.   ZIP/POSTAL CODE

IT'S YOURS FREE!

SAVE THIS COUPON

SDBP-1

IT'S YOURS FREE!

10TH ANNIVERSARY COLLECTION

FREE BOOK COUPON

It's Silhouette Desire's 10th Anniversary and we'd like to give you a special gift! Save this free book coupon. Six coupons entitle you to receive a free copy of Silhouette Desire's *10th Anniversary Collection*, three classic novels of love and romance.

YOUR NAME

ADDRESS

CITY   STATE/PROV.   ZIP/POSTAL CODE

IT'S YOURS FREE!

SAVE THIS COUPON